Vision of the Spirit Man

A NOVEL BY GEORGE MENDOZA

WISE TREE PRESS
Mesilla Park, New Mexico

Copyright 2022 George Mendoza

All rights reserved.

No part of this book may be used or reproduced
in any manner whatsoever without written consent
from the publisher, except for brief quotations for reviews.
For further information, write Wise Tree Press
at the address below.

Published by Wise Tree Press.

Wise Tree Press is an imprint of the
Wise Tree Foundation, INC.
P.O. Box 1243, Mesilla Park, New Mexico 88047.

Website: www.georgemendoza.com

Library of Congress Control Number: 2022934199

To my daughter,

Maria G. Mendoza

Author's Note

In 2011, I had a terrible hiking accident in the Organ Mountains in New Mexico where I live and dream my dreams. I fell a good thirty feet, broke my arm and my teeth. I suffered from cluster headaches for a long time after that fall.

I was lucky to be alive but the cluster headaches were terrible. I saw vivid visions which I painted and which turned into this story about Michael Spiritman. The headaches and pain somehow led to a wildly productive period during which I painted up a storm and wrote novels about my superhero, the spirit man.

One day the clusters stopped but I continued to paint and write books. I guess it's true that a good bump on the head can bring out the creativity! I have been accused of living in a fantasy and dreaming my life away. That's probably true, and I would not have it any other way.

Journey of the Spirit Man is followed by this book, *Vision of the Spirit Man. Heart of the Spirit Man*, a third installment of the Spirit Man series, is forthcoming.

Acknowledgements

I would like to express my deep appreciation to Erne Barge, Dr. David Boje, Louie Burke, Rachel Carrillo, the Castillo family, my art teacher Imelda Chacon, Bobby Cook, Mayra Enriquez, my sister Kathleen Firth, Dick Guttman, Janus Herrera, Neal Hidalgo, Anne Hillerman, Craig Holden, Dr. Dan Howard, Sonny Irizarry, Thomas Kindig, Doylene Land, Daniel Landes, Jamie Lapage, James McConnell, Michael Marrufo, my son Michael Mendoza, Monica Mojica, J.L. Powers, Robert Rivera, Ron Rowlett and his son Ryan Rowlett, Antonio Sanchez, Jane Seymour, Mary Sherman, Holly Watson, Marleen Wilson, Thomas Zubia and others who wish to remain anonymous.

I am very grateful to James Salas and Raquel Ortega with the New Mexico Commission for the Blind who funded this incredible book project. To Jessica Powers and Kathy McInnis who designed this beautiful book. To my agent, Frank Weimann, Folio Literary Management, New York. And to my editor, Shane Inman, the man with the magic touch!

A special thanks to New Mexico State University,

— *continued* —

the NMSU English Department, and especially the Creative Writing staff for their help and support in this and other projects.

All characters in this book are figments of my imagination with the exception of Michael Spirit Man.

George Mendoza
New Mexico

Chapter 1

The dream was hazy, indistinct, distant in a way that unsettled Michael—like all his dreams of late. He was in a mansion—or outside of one, somewhere in New Mexico or maybe not. Autumn leaves rustled at his feet or drifted over his head or else did not exist at all. The sun was rising, blazing its noontime glory, and setting all at once, and somewhere amid all of that, impossibly, the moon shone down and stars glittered on all sides of it. Michael tried to bring the scene into focus, strained to stabilize the desert landscape and place himself firmly within it, but to no avail. He heard a sound, muffled as through emerging from behind a wall of thick cotton, and it took a moment before he realized it must be a voice, a woman's voice, emanating from somewhere in this blurred world. He couldn't make out most of the words but he managed to pick out a name: Spirit Man.

Spirit Man isn't here, he tried to say. *I'm only Michael.* But his mouth felt full of something viscous and sweet—honey or molasses or something darker. He turned to find the voice and spotted a figure either in his study or beside the fountain outside or hovering impossibly at his window. Her form was as out-of-focus as her words. Every time he tried to identify something about her, it seemed to shift, slip out of his grasp.

Why can't I see? he wanted to ask. *Don't I still belong here?*

He made no sound, but the figure paused as if she'd heard his thoughts. She shook her head sadly and pointed at another shape, more distinct, more solid than the rest of the world. It looked just like Michael, sitting cross-legged in the sand, eyes closed. Spirit Man. He opened his eyes and met Michael's gaze.

"The way back is long, Michael," he said. "Are you ready?"

The pickup bounced hard over a pothole and jolted Michael

awake. He swore and rubbed his bleary eyes. The New Mexico desert whipped by on either side, sand and chaparral and sagebrush broken up by the occasional sotol stalk reaching for the cloudless sky. In the distance, a cluster of trailer homes gleamed, though the stillness of the place made Michael wonder if anyone lived there anymore. Sometimes people just up and left a place, or else were forced out by those who controlled the water lines, and their homes stayed behind, gradually becoming more and more a part of the desert.

Was Michael suffering a similar fate? Had he, too, abandoned or been abandoned by his dreams? Would he wake up one day and find he'd fallen into disrepair, that his decrepit self was slowly going back to the land?

"Finally awake, sleeping beauty?" Mark said.

Michael glanced at his friend, then back to the wasteland. Something wasn't right about this. Mark had died, hadn't he? Michael had seen it happen right in front of him. They'd been in a bar, there had been a fight, and Mark had been fatally stabbed. Yet here he was, in the flesh, the very same Mark he had known all his life, very much alive. Right, and they were driving to San Carlos for a weeklong vacation.

Things were starting to come back to him now, bubbling up from the amnesiac haze of sleep, but most of his present circumstances remained in those murky depths.

"Everything all right?" Mark said.

"Of course, yeah. Just tired."

"Aren't you always?"

Michael chuckled. "Certainly seems that way."

He wanted to ask Mark how the hell he was here, in this truck, speaking to Michael. The words danced on the tip of his tongue. But he was afraid if he spoke them, the universe would remember that Mark was dead, and he'd vanish right there in front of him, gone again in a blink. So he just leaned back and watched the land around I-10 unfold.

Almost five years had passed since his journey through the

  VISION OF THE SPIRIT MAN

dream world. He'd been so excited to return home back then that he didn't think until later about what he was giving up by leaving that world. He'd given up a place over which he actually held sway, a place that bent to meet him when he needed help, and bent away when he needed a challenge. He'd given up paradise, the riches of a pharaoh, and so much more. True, there were places in those dreams he wished never to see again, but the memory of those was so fleeting compared to the wonders he had witnessed. He missed the Spirit Lands and wanted more than anything to return. When he had first left, he'd assumed he could return whenever he felt the need. After all, he'd always been a vivid dreamer, always felt that connection to the part of himself that was Spirit Man. But since leaving the dream world, that connection had worn thin, his dreams had faded into the distance, and the gate through which he'd first traveled never reappeared. He had searched and searched the New Mexico wilderness for that gate, retracing his steps over and over until he'd carved a new path up and down the Organ Mountains, but all for nothing. He even tried praying, though to whom or what he wasn't exactly sure. (He'd never been much of a believer before, and his time in the dream world had only complicated matters).

Still, no matter how often he looked or how far he searched, he remained stranded in the real world. The realm of dreams was lost.

"Okay," Mark said, "something's definitely eating you. What's up? You know you can talk to me, man."

Michael shrugged and squinted at the heat haze ahead, hanging like smoke over the highway. "We just lose a lot of precious things during our lives, Mark. Sometimes we can get them back, some-times we can't, but you never know which is which until it's too late. That's all."

Mark nodded. "You sure like to wax philosophical, don't you? But I get what you mean."

Mark wore a black muscle shirt and his arms were so defined you could practically use them to teach an anatomy lesson. His body put even Michael's athletic frame to shame. Michael didn't remember Mark being so fit, but it had been five years after all.

His thoughts caught on that. Where had Mark been during these five years? Michael had the vague notion that his friend had been present, somehow, but he couldn't point to any specific memories, any specific moments. Mark's existence seemed to linger just on the edges of his recollections, teasing him with a face he *almost* recognized but just couldn't place. Again, he thought to ask, but decided a more subtle approach might be better.

"Do you remember the last time we went to San Carlos?" Michael said. "Must've been, what, three years ago? Four?"

Mark said nothing.

"And there was that guy. The really drunk Swedish guy on the beach, all burned to hell by the sun. Was that when you were with me, or am I thinking of a different time?"

Mark smiled sadly at him. "These things are best left unexplained, Michael. Let it be."

Something in the way he said it sent a chill through Michael, despite the blazing heat.

"Okay, pit stop!" Mark said. Though Michael didn't remember them taking an exit, they were pulling into the parking lot of a little diner out in the middle of nowhere. Empty desert stretched in all directions and not a bit of it looked familiar.

"Where are we?" Michael said as the two stepped out of the truck.

"Are you kidding? This is your favorite place!"

Michael squinted at the sign.

Wanderer's Cafe.

Dust blew across the sparsely-populated parking lot. Judging by the accumulation of it on the few other cars out here, they'd been stationary for a long while.

"You sure?" Michael said. "I don't think I've ever been here before."

"Would I lie to you, Michael? Your memory's just going, man. You're getting old." Mark laughed and slapped him on the back. "Come on, I'm starving."

They chose a table near the big picture window, where Mark could keep an eye on the truck. As expected, there were barely a half dozen other people in the place, all over the age of sixty. No one so much as glanced at them as they sat down. It felt like a scene out of a different time, somewhere Mark and Michael didn't belong. The same uneasiness he'd felt in his dream came seeping back.

"Welcome back, boys. What can I get you?"

Michael tried to contain his shock but, judging by Mark's smirk, didn't do a very good job of it. The waitress was Wendy, Michael's ex-girlfriend from what felt like another lifetime. Seeing her again brought it all back—the fight, the fall, Mark's death, the nameless illness slowly growing inside him. He tried to speak but couldn't. After a moment, Mark swooped in and saved him.

"Two orders of huevos rancheros please, and a couple coffees to boot."

"You got it."

She turned and walked off, laughing to herself.

"Man, you really made a fool of yourself there," Mark said with a smile. "Come on, it's not like you saw a ghost or anything."

Michael rubbed his temples. "Right, yeah, sorry. I'm just not feel-ing entirely myself."

"Perfectly natural. You're not yourself."

"What?"

"Or rather," Mark said, "you're half of yourself."

"What are you talking about?"

Mark picked up his napkin-wrapped fork and knife. "Okay, this is you," he said.

"Very flattering."

"No, listen." Mark pointed at the fork. "Michael." He pointed at the knife. "Spirit Man." Then he unrolled the napkin and let the utensils clatter to the table. The fork bounced once and tumbled to the floor. Mark looked from the fork to the knife and back again. "Not good, right?"

Michael was about to ask him what the hell he was talking about when Wendy returned with their plates—and an extra fork for Mark, as if she'd been expecting his accident.

Michael studied her as she set down their coffees. "What are you doing all the way out here?" he said.

"I could ask you the same question."

"I'm going somewhere. On vacation."

She nodded. "And where's that?"

"We're going…" Michael realized he couldn't remember. How could he not remember where they were driving? He'd known it just a few moments ago, he was sure of it, but now it was entirely gone.

"Wherever fate takes us," Mark said.

That was when the first bullet entered the café.

Chapter 2

Michael wasn't sure what to make of the hole in the window at first, the cracks like spiderwebs. In that first instant, he didn't connect the hole with the preceding bang, and sat puzzling over the peculiar image. Then Mark grabbed him as the second shot rang out and reality came hurtling back. The two dove onto the floor amid a rain of shattered glass as the shots came one after another after another. Each crack followed the last by almost the exact same interval. One, two, three, four....Tightly controlled, almost military. On the ground, Michael found himself face to face with Wendy, who had also hit the deck when the shooting started. Elsewhere in the café, people screamed, someone tumbled to the floor.

"Shit," Wendy said. "Oh shit."

"What's happening?" Michael said. It was a stupid question because he knew exactly what was happening, but he didn't fully believe it, and couldn't think of anything else to say.

The door burst open. At Mark's insistence, Michael crawled under the table and huddled against the wall, hoping the booth would conceal them. Too late, he realized Wendy was frozen, unable to follow. He beckoned frantically to her.

"Come on," he hissed. "Get out of the open."

More shots rang out, a scream was cut short, an old man's body hit the ground. A sudden wildness in her eyes, Wendy scrambled to her feet, ran toward the kitchen. She almost made it. She jerked once then collapsed, arms sprawled behind her. Blood pumped from the hole in her temple, soaking her hair and spreading across the floor. The killer advanced. From beneath the table, all Michael could see were his army fatigues and worn-to-shit boots. The certain, confident way he stepped across the bloody floor. Another three cracks rang out, followed by a ringing silence. Mark clutched

Michael's arm hard enough to cut off circulation, and his eyes brimmed with terror.

The killer seemed about to walk past their table when he paused. He turned. Before Michael knew what was happening, Mark lunged from beneath the table and crashed into the shooter's legs. He might've stood a chance if he had more momentum, or if the killer hadn't seen him coming. The man staggered back and three cracks announced the end of Mark's life. His body slumped, empty once again.

Michael couldn't stifle his gasp. Seeing his friend die once had been horrific, but twice?

"Come out," the killer said.

Michael shut his eyes tight and begged Spirit Man to come back to him, to join with him and help him get out of this. But he felt nothing, no greater presence within him.

"I know you're under there. Come out and let me see you."

Slowly, as if by a will other than his own, Michael emerged and stood to face the killer. The man had a shaggy beard and long, unkempt hair. A spatter of blood ran from one cheek to the other, his pale lips flecked crimson. He pointed his AR-15 at Michael and Michael was surprised to see that he was crying. Tears leaked down the killer's cheeks, turning his snarl into something more like a grimace.

"Why are you doing this?" Michael asked. He allowed his gaze to drift across the carnage. Everyone else in the diner was dead, bodies splayed across the floor or draped over booths, their eyes fixed in a final expression of shock and horror, their blood splattered on waffles and scrambled eggs and glasses of orange juice.

"I was lookin' for somebody," the killer said. "But he ain't here."

If any avenue of escape existed, Michael couldn't see it. Sure, he could dart forward, try to take the maniac's gun away, but Mark's bleeding corpse at his feet showed him how that would end up. For a reason he couldn't explain, his mind turned to every birthday party he'd ever had before his parents died, every race he'd run before his body conspired against him, every wonderous thing he'd seen in the dream world before it abandoned him. An end for everything. Was this his, then? Here, in a little diner in the middle of nowhere? Was this his final, irreversible conclusion? It seemed absurd, in a way. He was the Spirit Man. He had been to hell and back, had made friends with a pharaoh, had overcome the temptations of Paradisa. He wasn't supposed to die to some random lunatic. But then, neither was Mark. Or Wendy.

"You don't have to do this," he said.

The killer shook his head and another tear leaked across his ragged face. "It's too late for that. It was always too late for that."

Outside, the wind picked up. Heavy clouds rolled across the plain and beneath them boiled an immense wall of dust, all of it descending on the café. Lightning crackled through the dark clouds without ever touching the earth. A wash of sand, precursor to the dust storm, blew in through the shattered window and swirled around the two men as if urging them someplace else, trying in vain to pluck them from this mortal struggle and carry them off.

"There's still time," Michael said, shouting to be heard over the wind. He extended a hand.

The other man pulled the trigger.

Chapter 3

Michael Seymour ran without effort down a long, dark tunnel, toward a tiny circular light. If anyone had asked him, he wouldn't have been able to say where he was or how he'd gotten there or even why he was running. But he didn't have to think about any of these things because there was no one around to ask. He was utterly, entirely alone. Except for the light. The light grew brighter and brighter as he ran until finally it seemed to engulf everything, including his own body. He shut his eyes against the blaze and ran faster, legs pumping machinelike without a hint of exhaustion in his chest. Without warning, the light vanished, and he stumbled out of the tunnel into the day. He opened his eyes and shielded them from the sun. Where the hell was he, anyway? Waist-high grass rasped against him as a breeze rolled over the unfamiliar landscape. In the distance swelled a series of hills drenched in the deep green of their forest, and beyond those rose towering mountains, so tall their summits disappeared into the cloud cover. Michael turned to examine the tunnel he'd just left but it was nowhere to be seen. Just grass interspersed by lavender bushes.

He tried to piece together the events that had brought him here. The gunfire, the glass, the blood. Was he dead too? Or dying? Perhaps Michael Seymour, even at that very moment, lay bleeding out on the tile floor of the diner, dust from the storm covering his body like a blanket or a burial. He sniffed at the breeze, smelled the lavender on it, and broke into a grin.

"I'm back," he said to no one, to the field. "Aren't I?"

The grass stalks whispered against one another in reply. It was enough. Whatever had happened, he'd found his way back to where he truly belonged: the dream world, no longer blurred and indistinct but real, present, tangible. With this new certainty and a heart full of excitement, he set off in the direction of the hills.

The air was abuzz with insects, the soil was soft beneath Michael's footfalls, and the whole world felt achingly alive. As he climbed the first hill, he came upon a patch of wild gardenias blooming white against the lush green of the grass. Bumblebees bumped against the flowers and hovered here and there in a nectar-drunk daze. One rose to greet Michael, hung for a moment suspended at eye level, then buzzed off in search of its hive. Michael smiled and kept walking until he crested the hill. In the valley below, a family of deer picked at the grass along the banks of a silvery creek. The adults paused, sensing his presence, and turned his way, their noses twitching, big eyes appraising. Michael stood still, hoping he wouldn't startle the animals away, but they seemed to understand already that he posed no threat. They went back to their grazing as a breeze sighed down the hill. Trilling birdsong rose above the murmur of the creek. For a moment, Michael thought he could have stayed there forever.

Without warning, the pastoral calm was broken by a distant crash which Michael could have sworn was thunder but for the fact that the sky was blue and no storm loomed on the horizon. The deer darted soundlessly away and a second crash followed their departure. Michael searched for the source of the noise but nothing revealed itself. Something about the crash—thunder, explosion, whatever it was—unsettled him. It wasn't just the inherent threat it carried, though that certainly played a part. It was that it felt so alien in a place as peaceful as this. He had the distinct impression that whatever had caused the sound had come from someplace else, someplace not nearly as tranquil or pleasant as this. And, of course, if memory served, he was positive it wouldn't be long before he ended up in this other place.

Beyond the valley, dense evergreens overtook the land as mountains swelled from the earth, stretching skyward for thousands of feet before finally terminating in shining snow-capped peaks. Michael sighed and continued his long trek forward. Whatever waited in those mountains would find him sooner or later, so what use was there in wasting time?

As he began to climb out of the wide valley, he picked out a faint game trail and followed it through ancient gnarled cottonwoods interspersed with piñon and juniper. His path led him into a deep canyon, with steep sandstone cliffs on either side: ripped walls of ochre and orange sculpted by water and wind into bulges and tall, free-standing spindles, like sentinels watching over this crevasse. A bubbling little stream tumbled along the boulder-strewn floor of the canyon, and tall, solitary pines grew here and there along the edges of the creek. It culminated in a small pond of runoff water at the base of an imposing sandstone bluff.

Michael squinted up at the wall. Its bulk was submerged in the shallow, silvery-blue water of the little pond. A streak of rain-darkened rock bisected the cliff with the color of dried blood. In the center of this mark gaped the entrance to a huge dark cave—a black maw rimmed in gore. It had to be at least two, maybe three hundred feet up, but Michael knew, of course, that he had to find some way to reach it. Nothing was ever easy in the dream world, was it?

Weariness washed over him again and his legs began to ache, as if all the effort of his long journey had waited until this exact moment to hit him. The more he stood, the more they hurt, and the more terribly he wanted to rest, just for a short while. The thought of scaling that rock face, not to mention confronting whatever lay within the ominous cave, was not an appealing one. He sat down heavily against a sturdy pine. Some watchful part of him remained alert to a half-sensed danger; for long minutes, he imagined wild animals or giant mosquitoes lurking just beyond the rust-colored bluffs, but each second slid into the next, and still nothing sprang at him. Nothing but the creek stirred in the canyon. As far as Michael could tell, he was the only living being in this place.

The gentle burbling of the water lulled him into a deep tiredness and his lids grew heavier and heavier until, finally, he let them close. A short rest couldn't hurt, could it?

Before he had time to answer his own question, he was fast asleep.

When Michael's eyes fluttered open a few hours later, the world around him had grown dim and the air held the ruddy tinge of oncoming dusk. It was because of this change in lighting that he didn't immediately notice the figure in front of him, seeing it first as a gnarled stump of some sort. When he blinked the sleep from his eyes and saw it more clearly, he gasped and scrambled backwards on all fours. Whatever the creature was, it didn't look friendly. His first thought was that it was some sort of horridly twisted garden gnome, or perhaps one of Snow White's seven dwarves from a film reel that had been damaged in a terrible fire. A great bulbous nose drooped over thick, spittle-covered lips, behind which hid perhaps a dozen scraggly teeth. His shockingly blue eyes were only barely visible beneath his Roman centurion helmet, which was a little too big, battered, and had entirely lost its plume. The man stroked his comically bushy mustache and let out a tremendous, belly-shaking laugh, all the more startling given that it came from such a small man.

"What kinda soldier leaves 'is guard down in a place like this?" he said. "I coulda killed ya. Still could!"

Soldier? Why would this guy assume Michael was a soldier? He noted the short sword on the man's belt and the row upon row of ribbons and medals neatly ranging across his barrel chest. Unlike the rest of him, they were utterly stain free.

"Who the hell are you?" Michael said.

"I'm the one should be askin' that question." The man drew his sword and Michael crawled back further, quickly finding his back pressed against the cliff wall. When the man lowered his sword and started laughing again, Michael paused, confused.

"I'm just foolin' with ya," the man said. "'Course I know who you are. Everybody knows about the Spirit Man." He slid his sword back into its sheathe, then spit into his palm and extended it for a hand-shake. When Michael made no move to accept the gesture, the man wiped his hand on his tunic and laughed again.

"To answer your question," he said. "I'm Emmitt del Rio, Brigadier Sergeant, proudly servin' my twenty-fifth year of service under command of Cap'n Andrew Baylor. Lucky for you, we're on the same side this time."

"This time?"

"Don't worry yourself about that. What's important is that I need you to come with me."

Michael didn't feel especially certain about following the little soldier, and not just because of his tendency to spit. Was it really wise to just go traipsing off with the first dream world resident who knew his real name?

"What if I don't want to go with you?" he said.

Emmitt bristled and patted the pommel of his sword. "I don't much like to put it this way, Spirit Man, but I've been instructed to bring you back with me any way I can. It's nothing personal, of course. Orders are orders. But I think you'll find comin' along quietly is the right thing to do anyhow. Like I said, everybody's on the same side here."

"Same side in what? Who's on the other side?"

"Why, the war, of course. You been sleepin' at the bottom of a well or some such?" He raised his hand before Michael could ask any more questions. "Look, time enough for all that later. Right now we gotta get moving. I'm supposed to report back 'fore dark."

"Where are we going?" Michael said.

Emmitt pointed at the hole in the cliff and Michael now noticed a rope ladder dangling from it. "No more dilly-dallying now. Move it."

Emmitt led a reluctant Michael to the water's edge, where he'd left a worryingly small rowboat.

"Are you sure this will hold me?" Michael said, kicking the side of the boat. At least it seemed sturdy enough.

"Only one way to find out," Emmitt said. He clambered into the boat and picked up a child-size oar. "Now, give us a push and climb in."

Michael did as he was told, splashing into the water as he eased the boat off the shore, then hoisting himself inside. It rocked dangerously and for a moment he thought it might capsize, but soon enough it balanced out. Michael breathed a sigh of relief.

"See?" Emmitt said. "Nothin' to it." He plopped his oar in the water and started the arduous process of crossing the small pool. Michael peered over the side of the boat but could see nothing beneath the dark water. He didn't want to ask how deep this pool was.

The boat bumped against the cliff and Emmitt pulled it closer to the rope ladder. "Git on up there," he said.

Michael didn't see much option but to obey, so he hauled himself off the boat and started climbing. He felt the tug and twist of Emmitt following suit below him.

"What about the boat?" he said.

"Oh, that? Who knows. That's not my boat."

Once again, Michael bit his tongue. Some questions were better left unasked. He hefted himself into the cave mouth and found himself in a narrow, low-ceilinged space in which he could barely move without scraping some part or other on the rough rock. He turned back just in time to see the blazing sun sinking toward the horizon, throwing fiery spears of red and orange light across the landscape. The desert orange of the cliffs and the lush green beyond struck him more sharply than he'd expected. All this life force—boundless and beautiful. He had missed it dearly.

With a grunt, Emmitt hefted himself into the opening and blocked the light.

"Don't get too used to the views," he said. "Where we're goin', there ain't no beauty like this. Not anymore, anyway." He spat off the edge of the ledge then glared at Michael. "The hell are we waitin' for? We ain't got all day."

The tunnel before Michael was dark, damp, and uneven as it sloped down into the mountain. One misplaced step would send him tumbling down, probably breaking just about every bone in his body along the way. So, despite Emmitt's irritated grumbling, he took it slow, one foot at a time, bracing himself against the cave walls. The farther in he went, the darker it got, until he could barely see more than a few inches in front of him. He stopped and Emmitt bumped into his rear.

"What now?" Emmitt said.

"I can't see."

"What?"

"I said I can't see. It's too dark."

"Oh for cryin' out loud," Emmitt said. "I thought you could see everything with those magic eyes of yours."

Michael blinked. He had no idea what Emmitt was talking about.

"I have no idea what you're talking about," he said.

"Fine, fine! If you wanna be difficult about it." He heard Emmitt rummaging through his pack and half expected to be jabbed by some ghoulish device. Instead, Emmitt handed him a big metal flashlight, heavy enough to be a club. Michael flicked it on and squinted as the powerful cone illuminated the path ahead. Even with the light, however, the path still ended in darkness, and Michael wondered just how far this hole went.

"Happy now?" Emmitt said.

"More or less."

They resumed their trek. For a long time they walked in silence, and Michael got the impression that Emmitt was even more unhappy with him than when they first met—if that was even possible. As he walked, something else began to nag at Michael. The farther he went into the tunnel, the less he could remember about what had brought him here. Mark, the diner—it all felt far away, dreamlike. Like an old film he'd seen as a young child and had now mostly forgotten. On the surface, it didn't seem like such a bad thing to forget such brutal events, but something deep inside him told him he needed to hold onto his memories. Something told him he couldn't let himself become lost in the dream world as he had on his first journey, when he had nearly been trapped there forever. He wasn't sure which part of himself to listen to—the part which wanted to remember, or the part which urged him to forget.

"Where are we going?" Michael said, if only to break away from the tangle of his thoughts.

"Somewhere you're not gonna like, Spirit Man."

"That's very reassuring."

Emmitt snorted. "I'm not here to be your babysitter and tell you pretty stories. You'll see when we get there."

     VISION OF THE SPIRIT MAN

Finally, they emerged into a larger chamber. Stalactites dangled from the ceiling and huge clusters of stalagmites rose from the floor to greet them. As Michael swung his flashlight across the space, the light cast cruel, jagged shadows along the walls. He was about to ask Emmitt where they were going next when something moved behind one of the rock formations.

"Emmitt," he said. He pointed. "There's something back there."

Emmitt just heaved a deep sigh. "Boys! You gotta do better than that. We saw you right away! What happened to all yer trainin'?"

"Sorry sir," came a voice from behind the rocks. "We just got excited is all."

"Well you can come on out now. Lucky for you, our friend's comin' with us peacefully."

A group of about a dozen dwarves dressed much like Emmitt, but with far fewer medals and far more dust caking their uniforms, emerged from all around. They wore black hats, red bandannas around their necks, and big tall boots. Though the boots were clearly designed to come up to their knees, most of them had such short legs that there was nothing but boot between their ankles and their asses. Each dwarf carried an enormous cavalry sword in a scabbard festooned with braided cords, and each had a big six shooter pistol tucked into his belt. All looked at Michael in awe. They tumbled over each other to form up in front of Emmitt and deliver a series of clumsy, increasingly elaborate salutes.

"These boys are my Raiders," Emmitt said. "The very best of Captain Baylor's army. Long as you cooperate, you'll not be gutted and drained like a roasting goat, or otherwise inconvenienced. You hear, now?"

Michael grinned. "Trust me, I have no intention of resisting. I've very much interested in seeing where this goes."

Emmitt glared at him skeptically.

Michael raised one hand, as if swearing an oath. "Seriously. I'm just a little confused, and I'd really like to know more about just what on earth is going on."

"Well, there's your first mistake, see? We're not on earth."

"Great," Michael said. "That definitely doesn't leave me with more questions than I had before."

Emmitt, who Michael was beginning to suspect was immune to sarcasm, scoffed and turned to his troops. Even from a distance, they smelled like dust and sweaty feet and pond moss.

"Stubblefield! Hailey! Tolbert! Damn it all, Beerbarrel, y'all get your damn uniforms sorted out! Half of you are missing buttons!"

The scrubby little men patted their coats in horror, as if realizing for the first time how ragged they were. Michael began to laugh, but swallowed it once Emmitt wheeled on him.

"What's so damn funny, you damn giant?" Emmitt said, his beady eyes coal-hard and mean.

"Nothing, nothing, Emmitt," Michael said, struggling to keep a straight face.

"Good. Ain't nobody laugh at my soldiers and live to talk about it." Emmitt snorted and strutted around in a circle around his troops, inspecting them. Michael wasn't exactly sure what he was inspecting for, because they immediately started to jostle and hassle one another.

"Ya smell like old soup," one said to his comrade.

The injured party pushed him and said, "Me? I been castin' about for a clothespin to put over my nose since we left the barracks cuz of you."

"Shut up!" said a third. "You're all makin' jackasses outta yourselves."

"Oh kiss my ass," the first said.

"Ah-ten...SHUN!" Emmitt bellowed.

His troops fell silent and all hustled to fall into ranks, banging into each other, pushing and shoving to find their places. In seconds, they had reformed their line, their meaty arms and hands at their sides in knobby and gnomish approximation of military decorum.

"All right, now y'all listen up," Emmitt said. "Y'all probably know the Spirit Man has come to us from a far-away place. Real far. He done crossed over from one world to another to come give us some help." Emmitt paced up and down in front of his troops, his sausage fingers clenching each other behind his back. "Now, he done gave me his word he's comin' with us willingly, so there ain't no need to bind him up like some no-good prisoner." He paused to glare at Michael. "And he knows damn well if he goes against his word and tries to escape, we'll track him down, and it'll only be the worse for him."

The Raiders hooted and cheered, waving their pistols in the air. Michael looked down at the fierce crew and tried to smile, willing a trustworthy look into his eyes.

Emmitt waved a hand to silence them, then continued. "I promised Cap'n Baylor I would deliver the Spirit Man to him, and I am a man of my word." For a long moment, he stood there, regarding the rag-tag band. Finally, he said, "So let's get back to camp. An' keep your guard up. No tellin' what waits for us down below."

The Raiders saluted in unison, drew out their swords, raised them above their heads and shouted, "Hail to our Captain! Long may he reign! Yip yip! Ho-oh!" Then they began to march, stumbling often as they made their way over the rough terrain. Emmitt motioned to Michael to follow right behind them. He did so. Maybe, if he did everything they asked, he could eventually get these strange souls to trust him. Why were they so skeptical anyway? Weren't they in need of his help? He shrugged off his questions and hoped every-thing would become clearer soon.

The column of Raiders marched into a side passage just wide enough for two of them to walk side by side. The ceiling was so low that Michael had to duck to keep from bumping his head, though of course the soldiers didn't notice the inconvenience at all. Little by little, the cave floor changed. The uneven, bumpy surface gradually became shallow stairs carved into the rock, leading ever downwards.

"Where did these come from?" Michael said. "Did you make these?"

His words echoed up and down the corridor, and all at once the Raiders and Captain Emmitt whirled on him and loudly shushed him. Their shushes, too, echoed.

"No tellin' what's about," one whispered. "Best keep your mouth shut, ya hear?"

Michael nodded, a little miffed that no one had answered his question. Who were they afraid of, anyway? They were all well-armed and, despite their clumsiness, seemed like they could handle themselves pretty well in a fight. He kept this question to himself.

After a long descent, the tunnel finally leveled out. Here, at regular intervals, wooden beams held up the ceiling, as if it might collapse at any moment. Judging by the amount of loose debris on the ground, that didn't seem too unlikely. Michael shined his flashlight back the way he had come, but it was pointless. He had no idea where he was, or even how deep underground he was, never mind any concept of how to get out of here. His only choice was to keep following the Raiders.

Just as he thought that, Emmitt held up a hand and everyone stopped.

"We're here," he said.

Michael looked past the hunched shoulders and shaggy heads of the dwarves into the darkness of the cave. There was something in there—something barely visible, tucked away and hidden. He had to blink and lean closer just to make out what he was looking at: something like a small train, like you'd see at an amusement park or a circus. Incredulous, Michael realized that it was not a train at all, but a row of ore carts like the ones he had seen in the mines back home, in Silver City, New Mexico.

In the distance, Michael heard some kind of rustling and chirping, almost like a flock of birds approaching. The sound got closer, closer, and to Michael's horror, the darkness in the tunnel seemed to be advancing on him, blacking out his flashlight's beam as it approached. Then, in a fury of beating wings and echolocating squeaks, a swarm of bats burst forth, engulfing the small troop in a desperate, flailing bid to escape something. Michael cried out and covered his head as the little bodies flapped around him, occasionally grazing him with a wing or claw. The Raiders seemed entirely unfazed. Not only did they remain upright, they seemed to take great pleasure in the frenzy, leaping and shouting, trying to grab bats out of the air. One succeeded and proceeded to shove the entire creature in his mouth. A crooked wing stuck out as he chomped down and he pushed it back in, then swallowed the bat whole. He noticed Michael watching him and smiled gleefully.

"Try one," he said. "They're very nutritious."

"Protein's hard to find where we come from," another chimed in. "Always love a little treat, we do."

Finally, the swarm passed and the sounds of their fluttering shrank into the distance. Right about then, Michael heard what they'd been fleeing from. Another sound, coming from the depths of the cave—a clanking, a whiffing and chuffing, and the clink of metal wheels on narrow rails. At the sound, the troops began to cheer; Emmitt barked an order to get the mining carts ready.

"Let's get it on! Fort Huachuca Express coming up!"

Out of the darkness came the beam of a headlight, and soon a miniature steam engine appeared, its cylinders puffing like the endless rumbling thunder of a raging desert storm. A huge cloud of smoke roiled out of the darkness as the engine screeched to a halt on a big, round plate of metal right in front of the mining carts. The troops cheered again, and ran to grab hold of the engine and turn the whole platter around to point the engine back the way it had come. The engineer was a fat, jolly man, just as short and peculiar-looking as the rest. He wore a huge hard hat with a wide nameplate on the front: Conductor Hal Frisky, Jr. He blew the steam horn, letting off a long shrieking note.

"Hook up them carts, boys," he said.

The Raiders cheered wildly and clapped their stubby sausage-fingered hands together; they raced to secure the frontmost cart to the rear of the engine. Emmitt punched Michael's shoulder with one meatball fist and gave him a huge mustachioed grin. Clearly, Emmitt was very proud of the little steam train—proud indeed—so Michael did his best to muster up an enthusiastic smile too, though he couldn't help but worry about the safety of such a janky-looking vehicle.

"You got nothing to worry about now," Emmitt said. "Relax!" He stepped to the miniature train of cars as smartly as his short legs would allow, jerked open a small wooden door on one side of a cart, and crowed, "Hop right on in there, Spirit o' Man!"

There were just enough carts for the whole company to get on board. Michael climbed into one cart, feeling like an oversized kid in a wagon and hoping against hope that the ceiling wouldn't get any lower and knock his head off. Emmitt put his fists on his hips and let out a short, derisive cackle.

"I'll be right back, now. I gotta go pre-fright this train." He marched up and down the length of the rid, shouting orders and smacking his cavalry men on the backs of their heads, pumping them up for the journey. They were packed in four to a cart, with their sabers, their huge hats, and their absurdly tall boots jumbled together like so many ill-used toys in a box. The doors banged shut and the squadron cheered, hooting and yipping with excitement.

As the ramshackle crew prepared to embark, a few of the men unbuckled their wide leather sword belts and took off their dusty blue jackets, folding them up as pillows and curling up against each other so as to get comfortable. Emmitt walked alongside the train, checking the connections and the sides of the carts. Though the carts themselves were dark with a patina of ancient rust, the wheels were bright and shiny as stainless steel.

Like a dork at a used car lot, Emmitt gave the closest wheel a smart kick. Then he nodded in satisfaction, whistled loudly through his awful gray-green teeth, and yelled to Hal Frisky, "Ya ready up there, Junior? Ho-oh!"

The conductor hooted back from his spot in the engine car, and Emmitt hopped into the cart where Michael was sitting. He plunked down on the floor as the train began to jolt and whine, pulling the carts behind it.

"Hold onto your socks, baby! This is gonna be one hell of a ride!" Emmitt cried, as he took hold of both sides of the mining cart's frame. The cart began to rock back and forth, lurching and creaking as it descended into the darkness.

"Is this thing even safe?" Michael said.

"Don't worry! Be happy!" Emmitt said. As the little train began to pick up speed, the clatter of metal wheels and rusted carts on rail swelled to a fever pitch. "I never lost a man on this trip—not in over three hundred years!"

Michael gasped. "So just how old are you?" He couldn't quite make out Emmitt's face in the jittery light of his jostled flashlight, but he knew there was absolutely no way the sergeant looked a day older than fifty.

"Why heck, I guess I don't rightly know—six, seven hundred years, at least," Emmitt said. "How old are you, Spirit Man?"

"Well, I guess I'm twenty-six," Michael said, suddenly feeling terribly foolish about his youth.

A crooked wooden crate stood in the corner of their cart. Huffing, the gnarled sergeant hauled an oil lamp out of it and lit it, casting spooky shadows that fled along the rough-hewn walls of the mining tunnel like something out of a fairy tale. He held the lamp close to Michael's face and peered at him.

"Don't be ridiculous, Spirit Man. Why, you're older than I am. You just don't remember, or maybe you don't know it yet."

"What are you talking about?"

"Oh don't worry about it, I'm just a crazy old man, ain't I?" Emmitt burst out with a laugh so deep and genuine that, though Michael resisted, he could not help but join him. The two sat laughing, bumping along in the dim, golden light of the lamp, as the train lurched and hurtled madly through the dark.

Their cart was at the rear of the train and Michael faced backwards, so he could only see where they had been and not where they were going. He turned around once to look forward, but all he could see were glimpses of jagged rock in the pale glow of the train's little headlight, mostly obscured by the cloud of smoke and steam that stung his face. Eventually, the narrow tunnel widened into a cavern so large Michael couldn't see the walls or the ceiling. In the eerie flickering light, Michael saw the deep holes of abandoned mine shafts. He wondered, for a moment, what could be down there, in those depths even deeper and darker than the ones he himself had traversed today.

Suddenly, a huge explosion rocked the cave, accompanied by a blinding flash of light. The little train lurched and buckled; Michael slammed against the side of the cart and cried out.

"Saviors!" came a cry from the front of the train.

"Action!" Emmitt shouted. "Let's go! Get hot!" The dwarves drew their pistols and began blasting away into the dark, firing wildly in all directions. In spite of the lamp in their cart, Michael could hardly see a damn thing, and all he could hear was the deafening sound of gunfire exploding in his ears, and the whine of bullets ricocheting off the rocks and the iron sides of the carts. He grabbed his flashlight and tried to shine it into the dark when something heavy slammed into him, pinning him to the floor of the cart. In the glow of the lamp, he could make out a man, impossibly broad and muscular, kneeling on his chest. He wore black pants, a white shirt with frilly sleeves, and a camouflage vest. Michael couldn't see his face because it was hidden behind a plain white mask like that belonging to the phantom of the opera, except it was whole and covered his entire face. He could see the eyes, though, bloodshot and full of rage. Tears ran from those eyes in a steady stream, streaking down the mask and dripping onto Michael's face. The man, or creature, or whatever it was, raised its fist to pulverize Michael.

He wasn't exactly sure what happened next. Operating as if on autopilot, guided by muscle memory he didn't realize he had, Michael dodged the punch, kicked his attacker's legs out from under him, and, in one swift motion before the man had time to recover, brought the heavy flashlight crashing down on the man's skull once, twice, three times. The autopilot clicked off and Michael stood in shock, looking at the smashed, bloody head, the crimson spilling out onto the cart floor, and the red smears along his flashlight. He touched his face and realized blood had spattered there, too. He stumbled to the edge of the cart, braced himself, and vomited over the edge.

When he recovered, he still couldn't keep himself from staring at the corpse. The corpse he had created.

Emmitt patted him on the back and, with surprising strength, hefted the dead body over the wall of the cart. It tumbled along the tracks behind them, bouncing with a few sickening crunches before vanishing into the dark. The gunfire had died down by now. Raiders called to one another to make sure everyone was alive.

"You're actin' like ya never killed before," Emmitt said.

"I haven't." But even as Michael said this, it felt wrong. He couldn't figure out why. He was telling the truth, right? He'd never killed anyone before, never been a violent person. But that burst of violence had come so naturally, so easily, he couldn't help but wonder...had he just forgotten, somehow?

Emmitt chuckled. "Ya might think that, but Spirit Man's a warrior. He's killed plenty. How d'ya think ya knew what to do just there? If ya weren't a trained killer, ya would've been turned into a red paste, believe me."

"I don't know that I understand," Michael said.

"No need to understand, scamp. Haven't ya figured out by now there's more in you than some kid named 'Mikhail Seamonster'? It's fer the best. That's why we need ya. We're at war, Spirit Man."

Michael shook his head. Trying to figure out where he ended and Spirit Man began always gave him a headache, so he tried to think about something else instead.

"What was that guy anyway?" he said.

"That? Why, that was jus' a Savior. They ain't nothin'. More like pests than anythin' else."

"Is that who you're at war with?"

Emmitt scrunched up his face. "In one manner of speakin'. In another manner, not in the slightest."

Michael was beginning to wonder if he'd ever get a straight answer about anything from the sergeant.

"What's that supposed to mean?" he said.

"Means there's meaner things out here than Saviors, and far as I can tell they ain't the masterminds of all our problems." He tapped his head. "Not too much goin' on up here, if ya know what I'm sayin'."

The mining car lurched on through the darkness, once again picking up speed. The clackety-clack and groaning whine of its wheels and carts and beleaguered dwarven cargo grew louder. "Why do you call them that?" Michael said. "Saviors."

"People get crazy out here in the sticks. They start followin' some crazy cult leader or other and get it into their head that they're gonna save the world on the eve of its destruction, or some such. 'Course, we have a slight difference of opinion 'bout what savin' the world means."

The conductor let off a long blast on his steam whistle and Emmitt perked up.

"You're about to see what we're dealin' with. An' let me tell ya, it ain't pretty."

A faint gray light up ahead gradually swelled as the train chugged up, up, up from the dark. Finally, they emerged once more into the open air.

Michael gasped. It was nothing like the beautiful green canyon they'd left. The sky was a dull blue-gray, with a strata of dark, yellow-brown haze. If there was a sun at all, it was hidden behind the voluminous banks of dark clouds. The land itself was a wasteland. Black, shattered rocks, crooked dead trees grasping at nothing. Thick mist hung in deep hollows. Michael searched in vain for a sign of life—a bird or a bush or even a single green leaf on one of the petrified trees—but found nothing. All was dead and still. The earth reeked of marshy decay.

"Welcome, Spirit Man," Emmitt said, "to the Badlands."

Michael peered ahead. The tracks continued into the wastes which, if anything, became more barren farther along.

"What the hell happened here?" Michael said.

"It didn't always look like this. Used to look awfully like that green place where I found ya. It was beautiful, it was." He sniffed the air. "Sometimes I think I can still smell the flowers. Used to be wildflowers under every tree, 'round every hill. Animals too. Deer and foxes and birds of all sorts. Now that it's gone, seems like paradise in the ol' memory."

"What did this?"

Emmitt shrugged and gazed longingly across the badlands, eyes glazed over like he was seeing something that wasn't there.

"Don't rightly know," he said. "Not for sure, anyhow. Ya see, there was a sickness. In the land. Some folk called it rage, some said it was loss or grief, or maybe it was all of 'em mixed together. Whatever it was, that sickness spread. Just kep' sweeping outward, turnin' everythin' black, killin' every single thing it touched." He looked at Michael and the pain of this desolation was clear on his face. "We didn't have half a clue what to do 'bout it. We tried all sorts o' things, but nothin' worked. I don't think it ever woulda stopped if it weren't for the wall."

"The wall?"

"Look behind ya, kid." He gestured behind the train and Michael followed his hand. Now that the train had fully emerged onto the flats, he could indeed see the wall clear as day. It was immense, possibly the biggest thing he'd ever seen in his life. A huge stone wall towering at least a thousand feet over the landscape. It stretched in both directions all the way to the horizon and beyond. They must have tunneled under it on their way here.

"Whoa," Michael said. "Did you build that?"

Emmitt laughed. "Wish I could tell ya we did. But nah. Jus' like we don't know where the sickness came from, we don't know where the wall came from either. It jus' appeared one night, like someone dreamed it up, a giant circle to close off the whole damn place. Stopped the sickness in its tracks. I don't mean to sound dramatic, but I think it jus' might've saved all of Shook from becoming like the badlands."

"Wait," Michael said. "So if the rest of Shook is safe and alive, why are you all still here? Why not leave the badlands?"

Emmitt shook his head sadly. "Wish we could, Spirit Man. It's jus' a lot more complicated than that. You'll see soon enough."

The train trundled along, past outcroppings swathed in mist and gullies clogged with scrubby gray trash wood. Off in the distance, Michael could just make out a lonely soldiers' outpost. It had to be

Fort Huachuca, but it wasn't much to look at—just a collection of shoddy buildings made from gnarled gray wood, surrounded by a crudely-constructed stone wall. A rickety watchtower stood over all of it, though Michael couldn't tell if anyone was even manning it at the moment.

Long, shuddering moments ticked past as they drew nearer. Finally, with a thundering grumble, the train rumbled over an ancient wooden bridge which spanned an oozing flow of ruddy muck. A crude sign on a crooked post was jammed into the mud at the bank, and offered a generous appellation: West Fork River. The tracks curved to the left, traversing the rough land along the banks of a great puddle of muddy water. Michael noticed a few men who looked much like the Raiders stooping at the edge of this fetid pool. They dipped buckets into the water and started wad-dling with them in the direction of the fort. One waved as the train passed and a few of the Raiders hollered greetings at him.

Emmitt puffed out his chest proudly, his ribbons and medals glinting in the sullen light. "That there is Lake Emmitt," he said.

Michael tried to look impressed.

"Was it named after you?"

"No," the sergeant spat. "I was named after it."

Chapter 4

Conductor Hal Frisky Jr. blew the whistle as the steam engine ground to a halt at the Fort Huachuca Railroad Station, which was little more than a small wooden platform beside the tracks and a few stairs leading to the rocky ground.

"Let's go," Emmitt shouted to his troops. "Y'all clear out, now, y'hear?"

The crew of grimy soldiers jumped up and started tumbling out of the carts, tripping over each other's sabers and falling all over themselves. One man tripped on his way down and swung his stubby arms in circles in a vain attempt to regain his balance before falling. He looked, for a moment, like a drably-colored baby bird trying to fly for the first time. Michael was baffled as to how they had managed to fend off the Savior assault or even maintain a base of operations in such an inhospitable place for so long. Looks, he decided, can be very deceiving.

As Michael stepped from the cart, he heard a noise not unlike an approaching stampede. Shouts and hollers filled the fort as a crowd of at least a hundred Emmitt-sized soldiers came running toward the platform, tumbling over one another in their haste to be the first to reach the new arrivals. They seemed particularly excited to meet Spirit Man, but kept a respectful distance—though whether this was out of deference or fear, Michael wasn't certain. Soon, the crowd had formed a circle around Michael and were chattering amongst themselves animatedly, pointing and laughing and punching each other's arms. Try as he might, Michael couldn't pick out any words from the general hubbub, so he just hoped the things being said were good.

Emmitt pointed at someone in the crowd. "You there! Get us an escort to bring this 'ere Spirit Man through the Fort." A crew of six cavalrymen formed up around Michael. Emmitt nodded approvingly and led the way down the stairs. The crowd, of course, accompanied them, lifting clouds of dust as they made their way across a barren field. As they walked, the crowd jostled and stared, whispering and pointing. Finally a young-looking man worked up his nerve and punched one of the guards on the shoulder, saying, "Is he really the Spirit Man?"

The soldier kept his gaze fixed straight ahead. "What're you, daft?" he said. "Just look— he's so tall! If he's not the Spirit Man, then what in blazes would you take him for?"

The fort didn't look much more impressive from the inside than it had from the train. A walkway ran along the inside of the timber walls, dotted with old, rusted cannons. Michael noticed the barracks, nearly-empty storehouses, and the infirmary. Soldiers stood about in their ridiculous boots, arguing, laughing, and shoving each other about. Some worked at loading or unloading small carts filled with provisions, weapons, all the things a fort needed to maintain orderly operations. Others sat on crates, playing cards or dice, or stood around smoking pipes and spitting into the dust. No one seemed particularly ready for a fight, and it seemed that almost everyone on the base had joined the crowd to follow the Spirit Man wherever he went. Michael looked again at the watchtower and confirmed that it was, in fact, empty. He thought it might be a good idea to bring up this serious lack of security with Emmitt, but the mood around him was so jovial that he didn't want to disrupt it. Besides, they had held this fort until now, so they must know what they were doing, right?

Finally, the crowd arrived at their destination. It was not, as Michael had expected, any sort of command post or war room where he might get to speak with Captain Baylor and get some long-awaited answers about what was going on here and what was expected of him. Instead, Emmitt and his escort stopped in front of what was clearly a tavern. A wooden sign hung out front which read: "THE INN AT THE END OF THE WORLD."

Emmett turned to the crowd. "Spirit Man has arrived at long last.

                    VISION OF THE SPIRIT MAN

You all know what this means....It's time to celebrate!"

The crowd erupted in cheers and rushed into the tavern, carrying Michael along with the current of bodies. He had to duck under the door to avoid bumping his head, but once inside he was able to straighten up. The tavern seemed quite spacious at first—a rustic, simple place, wooden chairs and tables, a staircase on one end and a bar on the other—but as more and more people packed into the place it started to feel smaller and smaller. No one seemed afraid to go near Michael anymore, and they swarmed around him, patting his arms, shaking his hand vigorously, and shouting all manner of baffling compliments at him.

"Hell of a soldier, Spirit Man."

"We damn sure need a war bringer like you."

"I look forward to dying beside you, Spirit Man."

He didn't have time to process one before a dozen more flew at him, leaving him stammering thanks like an idiot. Luckily, the crowd was soon distracted by huge platters of food being brought from the tavern's kitchen. Fried sausage and sliced ham, rolls of warm crusty bread, wedges of cheese, bowls of pickles, and great urns full of the dwarves' favorite delicacy: pepper-spiced sauerkraut, deliciously salty and crisp. Horse-drawn wagons bearing barrels of beer were brought round, bungs banged out and taps rapped in, and soon everyone was eating their fill of meat and bread, drinking beer by the bucketful, and shooting their pistols into the ceiling. A band kicked up on a corner stage, beating on drums and playing frantic, magic melodies on flugelhorns and flutes. The soldiers of Fort Huachuca raised their glasses and their voices to belt out a discordant rambling tribute to the glory and honor of their fallen comrades and the ongoing struggle of fighting in the badlands. People kept pushing food and drink into Michael's hands and he happily partook.

After a while, Emmitt found Michael in the crowd (a simple task given his height) and slapped him on the back. "It's always like this when I come back with the boys," he said. "When you finish suckin' down that beer, we'll go up an' see Cap'n Baylor at Headquarters. Then when y'all get finished, us three'll rejoin the festivities."

Michael nodded and gulped down the rest of his beer, excited to finally have a chance to get some answers. On the way to Captain Baylor's office, they walked down the middle of what must have been the fort's best approximation of Main Street. They passed the general store, where large, hand-lettered signs were posted in the windows advertising the store's goods: bacon, tobacco, potatoes, cabbage, and so on. A barber's chair stood near the entrance to another shop; to one side, a fat brass spittoon glinted in the sunlight. These were followed by a silversmith, an apothecary, and an undertaker. Michael and the Sergeant walked up a couple of old, creaky steps, through two swinging doors, and into the Headquarters building itself.

The hall was quiet and empty. Emmitt's and Michael's footsteps echoed off the walls. Near the back of the dim space, a door opened and a furtive man, even shorter than Emmitt, emerged.

"Ah, Spirit Man, what a delight," he said, though his voice betrayed a nervousness that definitely didn't sound like delight. "I'm Lieutenant Eckles. We're so thrilled to have you here, but now is... well, maybe not quite the best time. Captain Baylor is very, very busy you see."

"Nonsense," Emmitt said. "Ain't nothin' more important right now than this soldier right here."

"Well you see, it's just—"

Michael held up a hand. "Actually, I've come a long way, and I have an awful lot of questions, so if you don't mind, I'm going to go in and see Captain Baylor. I'm sure he'll understand the interruption."

Eckles cringed, hesitated, then sighed and waved them both forward. "All right, come in then if you must. Just please try to be understanding."

The captain's office was small but tastefully decorated—at least, as much as anything in the badlands could be. A heavy oak table sat in the center, strange glass ornaments lined a desk against one wall, and from the opposite wall hung a painted portrait of Captain Baylor. Despite his diminutive stature, he was regal and proud. His uniform was spotless and he puffed out his chest to display his countless gleaming medals. His gaze was stern, intelligent, watchful; the sort of gaze Michael knew instinctively he could trust. Until his own eyes drifted below the painting to the real Captain Baylor, that is.

Baylor was slumped face down on the table next to a half-eaten bowl of chili. His fingers loosely gripped the handle of an enormous flagon and a puddle of drool had formed around his mouth.

"He wanted to get a head start on the festivities, you see," Eckles said.

"How long of a head start?" said Michael.

"Ah, well...about six or seven days."

Eckles patted Captain Baylor's shoulder. "He hasn't been sleeping well, I'm afraid—the burdens of being in command, you know."

Michael shot Emmitt a look but the sergeant only shrugged, as if he'd half expected this all along.

"If you come back later, he might—" Eckles started, but Michael cut him off.

"No, I didn't come all the way here just to leave with zero answers." He clapped his hands. "Captain. Captain Baylor. Come on, man."

With a groan, the captain stirred. He snorted, sucked in some spittle, and made a vague, ultimately failed attempt to lift his head.

"Huh? Whazzat?"

"Captain, it's Michael. Or, Spirit Man, I guess. You wanted me to come here."

Baylor made some noncommittal, non-word noises.

"In fact," Michael said, "you sent a troop of soldiers with guns to drag me here, so I would appreciate a few answers about why." When the captain's head started drifting back to the table, he clapped his hands again, right next to the drunk's ears this time. "Hey, focus up, Baylor. Why am I here?"

Baylor slurred something Michael couldn't quite catch.

"What was that? Speak up please."

"Ledder. I ro' uh ledder." He moved his arm as if to point at the desk opposite him, grew tired from the effort, and collapsed back onto the table. Before Michael could say anything else, Baylor began to snore.

Michael sighed and examined the desk. To his surprise, there was indeed a letter there, though he was certain he would have noticed it when he entered the room. He shook off the thought and picked it up. It was addressed to him. Michael glanced at the others, then peeled open the envelope and read.

"Dear Spirit Man,

Let me welcome you, once again, to the Mirror World of Shook. I hope your crossing was uneventful. The reason that you have come to us is quite simple: Our homeland has become a wasteland and the rest of Shook is in danger of following suit if we don't fight back. ———————'s armies are seeking a way to tear down the wall protecting the rest of our world from turning into more badlands, and I fear we cannot stop her alone. They are seeking someone named Annihilator, who has the power to bring down the wall simply by speaking their true name. You must find Annihilator before the Saviors do and destroy them so they cannot harm Shook. Our ancient homeland may be gone forever, but the same fate does not have to befall the rest of our world.

Spirit Man, only you have the power to stop ———————. Only you have the power to save Shook. You've done it before. I only hope we can count on you to do it again.

Help us, Spirit Man.

Signed,

Captain A. Baylor, Cav.

As much as Michael strained, he couldn't make out the name of whoever it was he was supposed to stop. The paper wasn't smudged, but his eyes simply refused to see the word. They skipped over it as if knowing it was not theirs to see. He held the paper out to Eckles.

"Who is this? Whose armies do I need to stop? And for that matter, how the hell am I supposed to stop a whole army? I'm not even a soldier."

Eckles squinted at the paper. "It seems," he said, "like this is something we're not meant to know. Sergeant Emmitt, would you care to take a look?"

Emmitt shook his head vigorously. "Don't be daft. Ya know I can't read."

Eckles handed the paper back to Michael. "I hope this gave you some of the answers you were looking for."

"I think it just gave me more questions," he said. "But I guess I'll take what I can get."

Emmitt punched Michael on the arm. "Don't worry about it, Spirit Man. It'll all make sense eventually. You just need some time to...process everything. Come on, let's go get a drink."

The sun was setting in what Michael presumed was the western sky as they walked down the dusty street to the tavern. Even before they stepped through the doors, Michael could tell the party was still roaring. If anything, it had actually ramped up even more. Shouting and singing and the sound of flutes drifted from the building, and a few drunken revelers had even found their way to the roof. They cheered as Michael approached, slapped each other on the back, and gulped down their drinks. He smiled up at them and pushed through the doors. The noise of the crowd washed over him like a hard, warm wave. Whooping and hollering men and women stamped in circles around the dance floor as a drummer pounded out a beat. Others danced atop the bar and only occasionally tumbled off. One man ran from group to group, toasting boisterously, drinking, then sprinting across the room to do it again with another cluster of people.

"You party now, y'hear!" Emmitt shouted, and he joined the dancing crowd.

Michael wasn't about to argue. He pushed his way to the bar. The bartender was an enormous, four-foot-tall man with a big, bushy red beard. He stuck out a big, hairy hand. "Hope you don't mind mah place! Needs a little fixin' but it's home to me!"

"Everyone seems to like it quite a bit," Michael said.

"Aye, you could say that. Now, what's your poison?"

"Whatever you've got," Michael said. "I could really, really use a drink right now."

"Well, lad, you've come to just the right place." The bartender plopped a frothing flagon in front of him. "This here's the strong stuff. Special keg."

Michael patted his pocket. "I don't have any money," he said.

The bartender laughed, pushed the mug toward him, then kept on laughing as he went to serve another patron.

One swig of the rich foaming brew told Michael that he should have started hanging out with this crowd sooner. He'd been missing out on the good stuff all his life. He chugged about half of the cold, malty elixir, banged the mug down on the bar, and burped with satisfaction. Suddenly a lot more jovial, he found himself joining in the general laughter all around him. He was never entirely certain what everyone was laughing at, but the important thing seemed to be that everyone was having a grand old time. When his mug was empty, Michael got a refill. When that was empty, he got another. Soon, he was feeling pretty thrilled about just about everything, and had all but forgotten his confusing, difficult problems.

Michael let himself be swept away by the energy of the crowd. When they sang along to a song he didn't know, he sang just as loud, trying to piece together the words as he went from the jumble of drunken sounds. When dancing erupted in the center of the tavern, he helped clear tables and chairs away and then joined in on the fun. Everyone seemed positively thrilled that Spirit Man was among them, laughing it up and dancing like an idiot.

But something began to change.

The more he danced and laughed and sang with the others, the more he watched the revelry unfold, the more Michael began to feel an inexplicable unease bubbling around in his gut. The general cheer seemed a little too easy, the singers sang a little too loudly, the dancers threw themselves a little too enthusiastically into each move. The laughter, too, didn't feel quite right. It was too loud and braying, too insistent on telling the listener that it emerged from joy and not something else. Soon, Michael started to sense that

　　　VISION OF THE SPIRIT MAN

there was something lurking beneath all this merriment, and that in fact the merriment existed to cover up this lurking thing. Behind every laugh, every smile, every song—was fear. All these people were deathly afraid of what tomorrow would bring, of what had happened to their homeland and would happen to them sooner or later. So they danced and sang and drank as if the world was ending because, for all they knew, it was.

Michael staggered off of the dance floor and braced himself against a wooden beam. He suddenly felt closed-in, short of breath. He felt these people's fear deep down in parts of himself he couldn't identify, and was all the more afraid because somehow they expected him to be their saving grace. Him, Michael Seymour.

Emmitt appeared by his side. "Come on, Spirit Man, need to get ya some fresh air. You're lookin' a little fuzzy 'round the edges."

"Huh?" Michael said, staring at him stupidly.

"Ya look like you're 'bout to pass out, son. C'mon." He yanked on Michael's shirt sleeve, and the two of them stumbled out into the street, careful to step over the lumpy prostrate forms of several snoring soldiers.

The moon was almost full, and so bright they could see their own shadows. The cool, open air was exactly what Michael had needed. He took a deep breath and tried to slow his pounding heart.

"Beautiful night," Emmitt said.

"Yeah, it sure is," Michael said. In the relative quiet, his own voice sounded enormous inside his skull. His head was still spinning, both from the alcohol (which he now wished he hadn't had quite so much of) and the realization that everyone was really depending on him to do something he had no idea how to do.

"How're the skies back where you come from, Spirit Man?" Emmitt said.

Michael had to stop and think about what Emmitt meant by "back where you come from." Since he had begun his adventures as the Spirit Man, he had seen many different kinds of skies, and at times he couldn't remember where he had actually started.

"Depends on where you're at," he said finally.

They stood there for a while, looking up at the sky companionably, in drunken silence.

"They really expect me to save them, don't they?" Michael said.

"You're the only hope we've got left, Spirit Man. The only thing we haven't tried. Everything else just..." He trailed off and the quiet returned. A cool wind whispered over the landscape and Michael wondered what it must have looked like when the land was still alive. He decided he'd rather not imagine this. It was too grim to think of all the beauty and life that had left this place.

When Emmitt spoke again, he did so in a voice so low that Michael could barely hear him.

"I think I know who Annihilator is. At least, I have a sneakin' suspicion which is a bit more than sneakin', if ya know what I mean. It's just that if I'm wrong...well, let's jus' say, I can't afford to be wrong."

Michael stared at the little sergeant. "You already know? Do you know where to find them?"

"I reckon I do."

"So you could end the war, right? Why wouldn't you do that?"

Emmitt looked up and Michael saw that whatever he wasn't saying must be causing him immense pain. He held it in his jaw, in his eyes.

"I'm jus' scared," Emmitt said. "'Cause I don't wanna be right."

Michael took another deep breath and let it out slowly. "Yeah, I guess I can understand that. Just tell me where Annihilator is and I'll do the rest. I'll put an end to all this."

"You're a good man, Spirit Man. A good man."

"I just do what I can."

Emmitt looked into his eyes and seemed about to speak when his face suddenly went pale. Michael whirled around just in time to see a huge man in a white mask leveling a rifle at him. Before he could react, Emmitt slammed into his side and sent him sprawling—just as the Savior pulled the trigger. A crack tore through the air and Michael flinched instinctively. He checked himself and realized he hadn't been shot, then rolled over and saw Emmitt standing over him. Blood bubbled from a gaping hole in his chest and trickled from the corners of his mouth. He looked right at Michael and mouthed what might have been *I'm sorry* before collapsing to the dirt.

As if on cue, a vehicular battering ram of twisted iron burst through the fort wall and charged directly toward the tavern. Dozens upon dozens of Saviors charged through the gap it had created. Somewhere, a soldier inside the fort sounded an alarm horn, but the call was cut short by the crack of another rifle. Michael scrambled backwards as the Saviors flooded into the town, hurling torches onto buildings and setting them aflame. The battering ram crashed into the tavern and a chorus of screams erupted from the building. People tried to flee as the whole building caved in. Some made it out, some were smashed by the battering ram, others were crushed or trapped under the falling debris. The invaders set upon the survivors as soon as they'd escaped the tavern, beating them with their huge fists, slicing them with axes and machetes, and shooting them full of holes.

The Savior who had killed Emmitt aimed again at Michael and his reflexes kicked in once more. Michael rolled out of the way of the shot, which pinged off the ground an inch from his head. Then he grabbed a loose rock and hurled it with such force that it cracked the Savior's mask in half. Beneath was the weeping face of the man who had shot up the diner. Only this time, he was weeping blood.

The image so shocked Michael that he didn't see the other Savior until it was too late. The man or creature or whatever it was, wearing an identical mask, grabbed Michael by the throat and lifted him two feet off the ground.

"You die now, Spirit Man," it hissed, before plunging a railroad spike into his heart.

The last thing Michael saw were eyes that he knew. Eyes full of pain, terror, and hate.

Then he saw blackness.

Nothing.

Chapter 5

Michael was dead. Again. But this time was different. He sat in a void and had time to think. Somehow, he knew that the void was offering him a very simple choice: Was he going to keep going or was he going to give up? He knew, of course, what the right answer was, but couldn't deny that there was a bit of a thrill to knowing the other option was right there, right in front of him. What would happen if he took it? What would happen if Spirit Man simply ceased to be? He shook off the feeling. He had to help the dwarves against the Saviors. Emmitt couldn't have died for nothing. Michael knew Emmitt had saved him so that he, in turn, could save Emmitt's people. Whatever was left of them after the Savior assault, that was.

For some reason, it didn't seem especially peculiar to Michael that, upon dying, he ended up in this place and remained very much conscious. There was no shock in the experience, no "wow, is this the afterlife?" feeling. The whole thing had a sort of distant familiarity to it, as if he had been here before many times, but very long ago, almost too far in the past to remember. Some part of him understood, without question, that the rules in Shook were different, especially for *people like him*—even though he didn't know, exactly, what people like him meant. What sort of entity was he, anyway?

As he often did with such seemingly unanswerable questions, Michael simply shrugged off the thought. It didn't matter, and it wasn't helpful to ponder this right now. He had a decision to make, and the answer was an easy one.

It wasn't in him to give up. He had to help, to do something.

The choice was made, and everything eased once more into total blackness.

When his awareness returned, Michael found himself curled in a heap in the dirt, somewhere new. The sun beat down on him, blinding hot. All around, scruffy weeds and stunted bushes dotted the flat, sandy plains. He struggled to sit up, nausea rolling through his guts as ripping pain began to throb in his skull. Gingerly, he brought a dirty hand to his forehead; it came away smeared with sticky, half-dried blood.

Carefully, he got to his feet and looked around. A vast desert stretched around him in every direction, dotted with scraggly, bone-dry shrubs. In fact, from a distance, they almost looked as if they were made of bones. In one direction, Michael saw a series of low, chalky hills. In the other stood a broad adobe and iron gate with nothing attached to it, as if it had simply been dropped there from the sky. Michael felt weak and his head throbbed under the bright sun, but his curiosity about the massive structure proved too strong to rein in. He staggered across the sand.

The arch of the gate was deeply carved with overlapping geometric shapes. If they were meant to form some kind of pattern, Michael had no idea what it was. Massive wrought-iron hinges fastened the iron door in place. The whole thing looked old, worn down, weathered by countless years out here amid the harsh, dry wind. Something about the gate struck Michael as familiar but he couldn't quite place it. He touched the metal and found, to his surprise, that it was cool instead of hot. He knew he had seen this before, crossed through this before, but whatever part of his mind held the memory was blocked off, inaccessible. All that came to him as he tried in vain to recall where he'd seen the gate was Mark's name. But what the hell did his childhood friend have to do with this strange obelisk? Slowly, he raised the hand-wrought latch. When he gave the ancient door a push, it creaked loudly, but swung open.

Beyond the gate was a scrubby expanse of desert—the very same desert in which he now stood. Some distance ahead, foothills rose toward the mountains, split by a zig-zagging trail. Michael laughed; somehow, for a single moment, he'd let himself believe something different might be waiting on the other side. Foolish, in hindsight. He stepped through the gate and a tide of déjà vu swept over him, nearly knocking him off his feet. He had done this before, he knew he had done this before—but where? And when?

Michael shook off the feeling, took a few more steps, and looked back. The door was gone, as if it had never existed in the first place. Somehow, Michael had known to expect that. He shrugged and continued walking.

All his attempts at remembering had dredged up something entirely different from what he'd been seeking: The wall, Emmitt, Fort Huachuca, Annihilator, the attack on the fort and the weeping faces of the Saviors. He needed to find someone who could lead him to Annihilator. He couldn't let Emmitt down.

As he walked, the sky transformed from pale blue to a swirl of blazing colors. The sun glittered, blue-white and painfully bright amid streaks of bright green and violet. A hot wind blew almost constantly across the sand, lifting clouds of dust in little puffs and plumes. Rolling dunes spilled into one another in all directions, but couldn't seem to stay put. Whenever Michael turned, he had an uncanny feeling that the hills had shifted positions. Not by much, but the more he looked from left to right, the more certain he became that the terrain was moving. The foothills, too, seemed further away with each step he took, their arcing lines growing fainter, not more pronounced.

Michael's gray shirt and dark slacks were streaked with dust and ash, but he couldn't even recall if they belonged to him, so he didn't mind too much. What he did mind was the heat. Heavy, inescapable. The farther he walked, the more he longed for even an inch of shade, and the more impossible that request seemed to become. Each time he looked back to see how far he'd come, he saw no footprints behind him. His face and hands were coated with a layer of fine silt, and his thirst was becoming unbearable. Each minute blurred into the next until Michael couldn't tell if he'd been walking for five minutes or five hours. The sun had remained perfectly still in the sky, harsh and unrelenting in its power. Michael's feet began to drag. Sweat drenched his clothes. His vision bleared.

Without entirely meaning to, Michael sank down to the sand and lay flat on his stomach. Coarse grains stuck to the cracked corner of his mouth. The sky above eddied with brilliant turquoise and tangerine.

"I'm probably dead," he rasped to no one. A mirage appeared on the horizon—a little café shot to pieces, littered with broken glass and chunks of plaster and dead bodies. Michael saw his own body among them, bleeding from a hole in his head. He closed his eyes. He didn't want to see that again, didn't want to remember it or think about whether or not it had really happened.

When Michael opened his eyes again, the sun was dipping below the horizon. The monstrous heat had been replaced by a cool desert chill. His thirst was worse than ever, but at least he could walk without feeling like he was on fire. Slowly, he struggled to his feet and kept moving.

After a while he came to a faint trail in the sand, an almost imperceptible line as if something had been dragged across the desert. With no better idea of where to go, he began to follow it, looking ahead into the fading light. The path unfurled in front of him, strangely untouched by the shifting flow of sand. As the colors swirling across the sky deepened to purple and navy, the temperature dropped quickly. Darkness fell on the shifting dunes and an enormous moon rose, blue-white like the sun, but cold and pockmarked and watchful. One by one, a blanket of stars flickered to life and the wind blew silvery streaks of clouds across the sky. When the clouds swept across the moon, a great shadow passed over the land, but within moments they passed, illuminating the sand in silver light once again. The dunes were purple-black, their edges crusted with white in the moonlight.

The temperature dropped even lower. Michael's thirst howled in his throat. His mouth was gummy and caked with grit and the taste of dust was driving him mad. His feet and calves ached. Raw blisters had formed on his heels and on the bony protrusions of his toe knuckles. He couldn't keep this up for much longer. He needed water and food. A clean bed and about two days of solid sleep wouldn't suck either. But he knew if he stopped, he might be lost in this bizarre, unreal place forever.

Michael stumbled over a shrub and dropped to one knee, feeling the weight of exhaustion and dehydration and hunger bearing down on him. With every shred of strength left to him, he forced himself to stand, to struggle onward. *Come on, Spirit Man.* The voice in his head sounded a bit like Mark's and a bit like his father's. *Keep going. Just keep moving forward.* One step. Two steps. *Keep moving. Don't quit.*

But on the eighth step, he sunk knee-deep into the sand. Before he could free himself, the dunes swirled around him and covered him waist-deep, then chest deep not a moment later. Panic gripped Michael and he tried to cry out, but the sand squeezed the very air from his lungs so quickly that all he could manage was a raw croak. Desperately, he scrabbled at the sand, but there wasn't so much as a twig to grab onto. By the time the sand reached his neck, there was nothing to stop him from sinking beneath it. No one was there to help him, there would be no indication that he'd even been there at all. He thought with horror of what it would feel like to be buried alive, to suffocate in all that sand. It was in his mouth now, up his nose. He choked on it, tried to spit it out, but only ended up breathing more in. It burned his nose, his mouth, his lungs as it went down. He thrashed his head about, utterly overtaken by panic. Then he felt his feet push through the sand and a moment later he was falling, falling through black nothingness, screaming in faint little breathless squeaks, flailing his arms and falling as though he would never stop.

He landed hard, with a bone-rattling thud, and the little bit of air that remained in his chest left him. He began coughing uncontrollably, spewing a cloud of dust with each cough. When the fit finally passed, he rolled to his side and wheezed in a shallow breath of musty, humid air. It was the most delicious air he'd ever tasted. Breathing had never felt like such a gift.

Sand choked his eyes and nose, streamed from his hair in rivers, and dribbled from his ears and out from beneath his clothes. His back and shoulders throbbed with the force of his landing, but miraculously nothing seemed to be broken. He yanked his shirt off and shook it, then used the cleanest patch to wipe the sand out of his eyes. It didn't help much.

All around him, inky blackness hung in the air, but in the distance, a faint golden glow pulsed gently. It grew brighter, and then dimmer, and then brighter again. Michael took another moment to recover and catch his breath, then he crawled toward it. Part of him knew he shouldn't. After all, what if it was dangerous? He was weak, defenseless, an easy target for whatever might be awaiting him. But where else was he supposed to go? He couldn't exactly wander out into the infinite dark—and besides, that didn't seem like it would be much safer at all. So toward the glow he went, hoping against hope it would be something friendly, perhaps something offering him a drink of water.

Small, sharp rocks littered the hard floor, cutting Michael's kneecaps and palms. Little by little, the dim glow grew brighter, larger. Then, without warning, the floor sloped sharply downward. Michael's wrists and elbows buckled, and he pitched forward, face first in the grit and gravel, and tumbled down the slope, crashing to a halt at the base of a huge boulder.

Michael struggled to sit up, shaking his head to clear the ringing in his ears. He looked around, dazed and battered. He was in some sort of cavern, but it wasn't like the one he'd visited with Emmitt. This one was vast and illuminated from within. The light he'd seen was much brighter down here, and he soon found the source of the light: all around the boulder he'd landed against, glowing chunks of amber were mounted in ornate metal fixtures. Others were mounted on the irregular rock walls, like sconces, and yet more were mounted on tall poles and fixed to the floor at intervals. They looked like torches but they didn't seem to carry a flame. The bluish light just emanated naturally from the amber cores. On the far side of the room, darkness clotted at the mouth of a low-ceilinged tunnel. Michael looked again at the boulder he'd struck and realized it wasn't a boulder at all. In fact, it was a perfectly rectangular block of stone positioned on a clearly manmade platform. The stone was carved with the same interlocked geometric figures as the gate he'd seen earlier, though he still couldn't decipher their meaning. Atop the stone rested a huge book. Suddenly Michael understood. The stone was an altar of some sort, though who had built it and what it was for, he couldn't begin to guess.

Michael struggled once more to his feet and approached the altar. The book, he saw, was open to a beautiful illustration of the landscape he had just left. Shifting skies, white hot dunes, a blue-white sun. Michael reached to turn the page.

"That is not for you." A voice rose from the tunnel—a voice of silvery whispers, like wind chimes and pan flutes.

Michael gasped and jerked his hand back.

"I'm sorry," he croaked. "I was just curious."

From the depths of the tunnel came a blueish-green, faintly glowing orb. It floated above the stone floor at roughly the height of Michael's chest. It glided toward him and stopped a few feet short of the altar.

"How did you come to this place?" it said, its voice shimmering in the musty air.

"I don't really know," Michael said. "I mean, I fell. I was up there in the desert and I stepped in—I don't know, a hole or something. I thought I was going to die. But then I fell through the sand and landed in here. If I'm not supposed to be here I can leave, if you just tell me the way."

The orb bobbed, the bluish light at its center pulsing, as if it were considering his words. Then, without warning, it darted at him. Michael took a step back but was too late. In an instant, the orb was everywhere at once, all around his body, engulfing him completely. From within, its blue light was painfully bright—even with his eyes squeezed shut it felt as though the light was penetrating his skull, sending a dagger into his mind. For a brief moment, he had the strangest sensation: he thought, *This is it, this is where I die,* but instead of just hearing the words in his head he heard them aloud, spoken in his own voice. At the same time, he could sense that he was not the only one who had heard this. Then the light moved away, shrank out of him and became once more a small orb.

"You are Michael Seymour. The Spirit Man." The being's voice seemed to vibrate up from Michael's own chest.

"I am," Michael said. "But what are you? A...spirit? Some kind of angel?"

"We are the Light," the orb said, and this time it seemed to possess many voices, as though each note of the wind chime was the voice of a distinct being.

Michael nodded. "Okay. And you live here? In this cave?"

"We are the guardians of the Book." The orb's many voices echoed through the cavern. *Guardians of the Book. The Book, the Book. Guardians of the Book.*

Michael glanced over at the huge leather-bound volume on the altar. Slowly, the orb floated toward it, coming to a stop just above its pages.

"Come," the orb whispered. "We have something for you, Spirit Man."

We have kept it safe for a millennium. It is for him.

We have what he seeks.

We have truth for the Spirit Man.

The voices grew louder, more insistent. Michael looked again at the book; within its pages, the dunes and the brilliant hues of the sky began to move.

Chapter 6

Michael gasped as the light from the orb changed from aqua-marine to pure, clear, blinding white, then dimmed down to more comfortable level. Rust-colored dunes crawled and slid on the page before him, like a collection of worms in a bowl. Above the dunes, the sky swirled with brilliant colors, streaked with shining gold. Slowly, the swirling became more and more consistent as streaks of color aligned and began to move together, twisting in a clockwise circle. Michael couldn't do anything but watch, utterly entranced. A pinprick of black appeared in the center of the swirl. Little by little it grew and little by little Michael felt himself being drawn down into it, until the black space was all he could think about and all that he could see.

Gaze upon this Truth, Spirit Man. We kept it safe for you.

Deep in the darkness, a speck of gray winked into being; suddenly it zoomed into focus, filling Michael's vision with the inside of a prison cell.

The grim little room was uncomfortably hot. No window, just a solid metal door. Solitary confinement. The floor was plain concrete and the walls were the same. A rust-stained sink was bolted to the wall beside an ancient, crooked toilet. The stench that rose from it was partly the smell of shit and partly that of rot, mixed with the wet clay smell of old, badly done plumbing. And against one wall, the man who had shot up the diner lay on a narrow cot.

Michael's blood ran cold. Here was the man who had murdered his best friend in cold blood, and gunned down countless others right in front of him. Here was the man who...who...Michael tried to recall whether this killer had pulled the trigger on him as well—blown him away like all the rest—but he couldn't say for certain. All he knew was the deep well of hate which bubbled inside him as he looked at the sad, gaunt form lying curled in the fetal position on his cot. Michael's first instinct was to glance around for a weapon, something he could use to punish this monster. He didn't even question this instinct. It seemed only right and just to want only to inflict pain and misery on someone as wretched as this.

His name is Joey. Joey Evans.

Michael looked around for the source of the voice but couldn't find it.

"I don't want to know that," he said. "I don't care what his name is."

His name is Joey.

Michael was about to say something else when he heard footsteps approaching. Joey must have heard them too, because he raised his head a little. His eyes were bloodshot and sunken. His hair appeared to have been falling out in clumps. His face was gray and hollow.

The metal hatch on the bottom of the door slid open and a guard pushed a tray through.

"Lunch, asshole."

The hatch slid shut. Joey went to the door and took the tray without a word, than sat at the end of the cot to eat. The soup looked greasy, filled with potatoes and somewhat questionable meat. It came with a cup of water and a piece of rock hard toast. Michael could hear the crunch with each bite as Joey ate the toast and drank the murky water. Joey took a few sips of the soup, grimaced, and then put the tray on the floor and lay back down on his cot. The air in his little cell was stifling, layered with odors from the soup and sweat and shit. Rivulets of sweat rolled down Joey's forehead and onto the already yellow-stained pillow. Nevertheless, he hugged himself as if freezing. He stared at the wall, rocked, and started to hum a tune so badly off-key Michael had no idea what it was.

"You son of a bitch," Michael said. "You crazy bastard. I hope you rot in here for the rest of your filthy life."

As if he'd heard Michael, Joey suddenly sat up. Michael took a step back as Joey looked around but the killer still didn't seem to see him at all. Instead, Joey sprang to his feet and flung himself against the metal door. Michael watched in horror as he began to beat his head against the metal.

Thud. Thud. Thud. A smear of blood appeared on the gray paint. Rhythmically, incessantly, Joey bashed his skull against the door—*thud thud thud*—and the stain grew with each and every blow. Finally the guard's voice sounded from the hallway outside.

"Knock that shit off, asshole! Right now!"

Thud. Thud.

"I'm not playing, you sick freak. Cut it out, or so help me, you'll spend the rest of your worthless life in a strait jacket."

Thud. Again and again, Joey cracked his head against the steel, like a man possessed. In spite of the violence of the blows and the now-significant quantity of blood on his face and on the door, Joey showed no sign of losing consciousness or even tiring.

Thud. Thud. Thud.

Two burly guards flung the cell door open, shoving Joey back. They charged him and pinned him against the far wall. Then the thinner of the two jabbed a syringe into Joey's bicep. In seconds, Joey's eyes glazed over and he slumped into their arms, almost childlike in that moment. The guards dumped him on the cot and secured his wrists and ankles to its iron frame with zip ties.

"Let the night shift deal with him," one guard said. Then they left, and Joey was once again alone in his cramped, stifling cell.

"At least he's suffering," Michael said, though whether to the orb or to himself he wasn't sure. "He's being punished for what he did. He's suffering for taking those poor people's lives."

Do you really think that's what the Book wanted you to see? Do you really think that's what the Book wanted you to learn?

A thin finger of blue light seeped under the door, followed by another. Slowly, the light coalesced into the orb, hovering in the room beside him. It grew brighter and began to expand, once more engulfing Michael. This time, however, it engulfed Joey as well.

The hatred inside Michael surged, more powerful than ever before. Anger. Pain so intense that he gritted his teeth and bit into his lip until it bled, just to feel a different pain for a single instant. But underneath all of that was a bottomless pit of grief, of sorrow,

     VISION OF THE SPIRIT MAN

of utter wasting despair. All was lost. All had always been lost. He reeled from the awfulness of it, his stomach churning. Bile rose in his throat and he retched but produced nothing. Blood pounded in his temples.

Gradually, Michael began to understand where all this was coming from. This was Joey. Michael was feeling what it was like to be Joey all the time, every day, every night, always. He felt like he was suffocating and all he could think to do was lash out at anything and everything around him like a dying animal. Somewhere in this deep black cloud, he was aware of the monstrosity of the things he had done, the inhuman wretchedness of his actions—but that understanding was buried deep, barely accessible. All he really knew was pain.

Michael whimpered and tried to back away from the incessant light that hurt so much, desperate to escape the horror contained within. Finally, the blue light withdrew. With it vanished the cell, the cot, the smell, and Joey. Michael found himself once again standing at the altar, resting his palm on the Book. The orb bobbed in front of him.

"You are correct," it said. "He suffers."

Michael nodded, still too shaken to speak.

"His prison is within. It was before and will continue. It will never leave him. His life is empty of any light and always will be."

It paused, shimmered, continued.

"Does this satisfy you? If he were made immortal, doomed to linger in this agony for all eternity, would that satisfy you? Do the demands you make with your hate bring any life back to his victims, and solace to their friends and families? Does inflicting pain cure others of pain?"

Michael stared at his hands, remembering the violence they had inflicted upon the Savior in the minecart. Blow after blow, blood spattering his face.

"No," he said. "I think I understand."

"Emmitt and his Raiders believe Spirit Man is a warrior, sent to destroy. This is not correct. Spirit Man is a builder, sent to restore."

"I don't want to hurt people," Michael said.

"You will have to. But not for vanity's sake, as with Joey. You must only cause harm in service of a larger good, in service of healing the land and its inhabitants."

"How do I know? How do I know what fights are worth fighting?"

"Let your spirit guide you. You have become distant from it of late but the Spirit Man is still within you, inextricably a part of you. Listen to him when you feel doubt."

Michael nodded. His mouth was dry, his bones felt heavy.

"Our time is nearing its end, Michael Seymour. But remember: though death surrounds you, it is not stronger than life. Life persists, prevails—if only you let it."

"I'm not sure I understand," Michael said.

"You will, when the time is right. Now, let us go."

Chapter 1

The orb floated toward the tunnel, into its inky depths. Its light revealed a rough stone staircase that angled upwards. Without a second thought, Michael followed the light, climbing as quickly as his tired legs would allow. Behind him, the altar's glow slowly faded into nothingness.

The cool, dank air grew drier with each step, and the orb's light grew less intense. Finally, the staircase curved sharply to the right and the tunnel widened to reveal the exit. Beyond it, the desert sky glowed with swirling shades of blue and purple. The dunes were blood red, tinged silver at their peaks by the light of a piercingly brilliant moon.

The orb paused just before the exit.

"You are weary, Spirit Man. We can go no further, but we offer you a great gift before you leave." The voice echoed gently off the rough stone walls.

"A gift? What kind of gift?" He wasn't sure he could take another vision like the one the Book had given him.

"Close your eyes, Spirit Man."

Despite his apprehension, Michael did as he was told. Instantly, he felt a dull heat pulsing inside his skull, throbbing with a dull, slow energy behind his eyes. The pulse grew stronger and brighter with each second. Soon it became almost a miniature sun stuck inside his head. Michael whimpered as the heat grew almost unbearable. It felt as though someone was pouring hot oil into the middle of his brain. He dropped to his knees on the stone steps, grasping his skull with shaking hands. Strangled groans ripped from his throat, and still the glowing, pulling heat throbbed on and on. Finally, the energy began to recede. He opened his eyes slowly, unsure he would be able to see again at all, and saw the orb floating calm and sure just a hair from his face, its light as cool and as blue as ever.

"You have great strength, Spirit Man."

"What did you just do to me? What was that all about?"

"Calm your spirit, Spirit Man. Concentrate and see. We have given you a great gift."

Michael steadied his breathing, closed his eyes again and counted to twenty, focusing on slowing his heart rate. The warmth in his skull lingered, like a faint aftertaste of something spicy. When he opened his eyes, everything was different.

Before him the orb floated, a cool blue-green, but now Michael could perceive the faintest shadow of an expression hidden in its light. Not a face, per se, but something like the memory of a face, or the echo of it. Its faint, half-sensed features shifted and swirled within its low blue light, multiplying and rejoining: one face became many, then many became one. Michael gasped.

The orb breathed out a tinkling little chuckle. "Now you can see us as we truly are. Look to the desert. Concentrate."

Michael focused and looked across the dunes. The once-dark sand sparkled with millions of brilliant twinkling lights, as though permeated with tiny chips of diamonds. Tiny, iridescent plants which he had not before seen lifted their delicate leaves into the air.

"Holy shit," Michael said.

The orb pulsed, a contented sigh of sorts. "This is our gift. It will serve you well, Spirit Man, in ways you may not expect. Have courage, and remember what you have learned here." The orb's voice split and echoed, becoming many different voices chanting in magical unison.

"The path is long."

"But your spirit is powerful."

"And now, you see."

"There is darkness."

"There is death."

"Yet..."

"There is light."

"There is life."

Michael nodded solemnly. "Thank you," he said.

The many voices collapsed and condensed into one.

"Go now, Spirit Man. Resume your journey. Find the City of Dreams." Then the light of the orb retracted and the orb floated serenely back down the stone steps. Its glow gradually faded from the walls until the tunnel was once again filled with blackness.

Michael stepped out into the desert night. His thirst felt unimportant amid the glittering dunes, as did his exhaustion. The world had been renewed and he had been renewed along with it. The shifting of the landscape which he had at first interpreted as random now struck him as deeply meaningful. The sands shifted with a rhythm, a musical language which escaped his understanding but was no less beautiful for it. The sky swirled, huge and expansive and rich with stars. The enormous moon watched over the desert as a mother watches her child. Michael brushed the leaves of one of the sprouting iridescent plants and they quivered as if fully alive and aware. For the first time since arriving in the desert, Michael smiled. Then he began walking.

At first, as before, he had no real idea where he was going. But slowly a new path began to reveal itself, this time through the glimmering shards embedded in the sand. Some of them shone more brightly in the moonlight, pointing the way through the dunes.

He wondered how long he had been out here—and how long the soldiers in the badlands had been fighting for their lives. Were they still fighting? Had anyone survived the Savior assault on their fort? Wherever he was going, he needed to get there soon. Too many people were counting on him for him to remain lost forever. The orb had mentioned a place called the City of Dreams, but Michael had never heard of such a place, and had to admit he had absolutely no idea where to find it. All he could do was follow the shining path and hope it would lead him there.

Slowly, the sun rose over the desert. The shimmering dunes changed once more to a rusty copper color, their brilliance hidden once the moon and stars were banished from the sky. Somehow, though, Michael still knew the route he needed to follow, as if he could still see it on a wavelength of light not perceptible by his conscious mind. With the sun, the heat too returned, and reminded him of his crippling thirst. He couldn't make another trek like he had the day before—that much was certain. He would dry up until he was nothing more than a desiccated husk, a mummy without its funeral wrappings. Then the hot desert wind would turn him to dust and blow him away, scatter him across the dunes as if he had never been there at all.

The grim musings put a strange thought in his head. What if it wasn't just a flight of fancy? What if these dunes actually were the remnants of dead, dried-up beings? Somewhat to his surprise, he didn't find the thought especially horrifying. Weren't there invisible plants emerging from this sand, after all? If this was a place full of death, it was just as much a place full of life.

By midafternoon, the sun had baked his face and arms to a painful, deep red, but he finally saw something which broke up the endless, unchanging monotony of the dunes. In the distance lay a jagged outcropping of yellowish stones, flanked on both sides by the red-orange sand of the desert. The ridge stones were streaked with blood red, ochre and black. Here and there among their many angry cracks and crevices, scraggly brownish weeds ruffled and waved in the hot desert wind. The invisible path led straight up the rocky ridge, as if something awaited Michael at the top. Steeling himself against the heat, he marched to the ridge and began to climb. The rocks were blazing hot and burned his palms as he scaled them, but he wouldn't be dissuaded. One hand after the other, one foot after the other, he crawled up the steep incline and finally reached the top.

He had hoped to see some lush oasis beyond, but it was not to be. On the other side of the ridge lay a vast valley of sand, shimmering and distorted by the heat. The terrain was rough—scraggly outcroppings of rock punctuated by pockets of sand. Ugly thorn bushes clung to life here and there. Far below, Michael spotted a rattlesnake, curled in the meager shade at the foot of a dark brown boulder. But there, in the center of the valley, was something different.

It was a green patch—hardly bigger than a postage stamp from this distance, but it stood out among the unending acres of barren sand and stone. Michael closed his eyes and took several deep breaths, searching the depths of his mind for the special vision the orb had given him. When he opened his eyes, the little postage stamp of green glowed sharp and vivid, as though it was teeming with life. Life and greenery could only mean one thing: water. Michael hurried down from the ridge, energized by the prospect of quenching his long-neglected thirst. He could almost taste the water as he hustled across the sand; so cool and crisp and pure, perhaps with just a hint of desert minerals. He could practically feel it on his tongue, feel it running down his throat, soothing his parched vocal cords. With the near-certainty of water came the near-certainty that everything would be all right after all. He would find the City of Dreams—of course he would. He would find and stop Annihilator. He would save Shook from the fate which had claimed the badlands. Trudging across that valley, Michael wondered why he had ever doubted himself at all.

It took nearly two hours before Michael finally reached the narrow swath of green. Verdant grasses rose nearly ten feet high, swaying in the wind. In the center of the grasses, a large path had been trampled down by someone, or something. Michael peered at the path, which snaked ahead and disappeared around a curve. Well, nowhere else to go, he figured. Besides, maybe the path had just been by some harmless animal seeking the same water he was now after. With a shrug of resignation, he walked into the tall grass.

Soon he came to a small clearing. A well was sunk in the center of it, surrounded by round white stones. Michael looked around the clearing, amazed. A small wooden sign was mounted on a rough-hewn stake near the well.

"Drink, traveler," it read in blocky, ill-formed letters.

Michael wondered for a moment if this could be some sort of trap, designed entirely to capture thirsty travelers like himself. But his thirst quickly overwhelmed those worries. Between dying of dehydration and dying to some absurd trap, he decided he would much prefer the latter. At least it would be quick.

He stumbled to the well, hauled the bucket up on its slimy rope, and drank greedily, scooping water up in his cupped hands, slurping it down and splashing it over his face and head gleefully. The water was fresh and cold in his parched throat, so cold it stung against the sunburned skin of his arms and neck. He took off his filthy shirt and shook it out as best as he could, releasing a thick cloud of sand into the hot, dry air. Then he submerged it in the bucket, swished it around, and used it to wipe the streaks of dust off his shoulders and chest. When the water in the bucket was dark gray-brown with dirt and sweat, he dumped it into the grass and hauled up another. He submerged his head and drank as much as he could, until his belly felt ready to burst, then wiped the dust out of his ears and rinsed his shirt again.

With his thirst finally quenched, Michael stood up and began to explore the little clearing. Dozens of shallow springs dotted the area—natural pools bordered by dull yellow flagstones. The springs seemed natural, but the stones certainly were not. Someone had brought these from somewhere else and placed them here, though he couldn't figure out why. What use was there in landscaping a tiny oasis in the middle of a completely uninhabited desert? He roamed from one spring to the next, gazing into the burbling waters. His new, more sensitive vision revealed an astonishing ecosystem of tiny creatures swimming and swirling in each spring. Some resembled creatures he recognized, like seahorses and tiny, squirming starfish, while others were little more than undulating blobs of goo—irrefutably alive, yet primitive, protozoan. He watched the microscopic critters floating around and began to see, as with the shifting of the dunes, a distinct pattern in their movements. Though he couldn't decipher it, he sensed deep in his gut that even the smallest twitch of a starfish's limb had some sort of grander purpose, as if all these living things fit into a vast and incomprehensible system of the universe. It occurred to Michael that he, too, might fit into this system. Perhaps that was why he saw the path laid out before him. Perhaps all these little aquatic critters saw similar paths in their own way, and knew instinctively that they needed to follow them.

Michael made his way to the edge of the clearing, where he found a huge white tub. It was buried up to the rim in sand and almost entirely hidden by the shaggy grass. The tub was made of pure white porcelain, with beautiful blue and yellow tiles running along the inner edge. Strangely, it seemed almost brand new, barely damaged or worn by the harsh elements at all. Clearly, someone had put this here quite recently. Probably the same someone who had put effort and creativity into building this sanctuary in the desert. Even more peculiar—and a little worrying—was the fact that the tub was full of clear, steaming water. Michael looked closer and realized that the drain was actually linked up to a hot spring, from which fresh, hot water constantly bubbled.

He looked around furtively. In the distance, the sharp ridge of stones loomed, harsh and jagged like the spine of some terrible beast. Elsewhere, he could see nothing but the thick, tall grass. He listened for any sound other than the wind and the shuffling whispers of the grass but heard nothing. As far as he could tell, there was not another living soul for miles.

Michael slipped off his torn clothes and slid into the hot spring. The water soothed his aching bones and muscles. Gradually, the sand that had become caked in his every sweaty crease loosened and floated free. The feeling of being submerged in these cleansing, healing waters was heavenly. He'd never imagined such a simple thing could be so precious and wonderful. He closed his eyes and let his mind drift, breathing in the miracle of steam. He was exhausted, his memories a tangled mess of half-formed images: fighting and killing, running, dying....He wished he had asked the orb about that last one, but knew he probably wouldn't have gotten a straight answer anyway. There were certain things about this place he needed to just accept and stop asking questions about, because he'd probably never get the answers.

He must have dozed off in that soothing water because when his eyelids slowly slid open the sun was resting on the western horizon. He watched the steam from the tub drift up as if caressing the sun, soothing it, too, so it could rest for a while. Michael sighed, basking in his deep contentment. All his bodily ills had simply vanished while he rested. Some property in the water had cured him even of his sunburns. He could stay here forever, if he had no place else to be.

But he did, of course. The City of Dreams awaited him, as did the residents of the badlands and whoever it was they called Annihilator. With a groan, Michael raised himself out of the tub and pulled his clothes back on.

No sooner had he done this than the red hills that surrounded the valley began to tremble ever so slightly. The valley floor remained still and silent, but Michael sensed that something was approaching from the ridge, and he had a pretty good guess as to what it was.

Michael's suspicions were confirmed when dozens of Saviors spilled over the ridge and began clambering down the slope into the valley. They charged across the valley floor, heading straight for him.

"Well, time to go, I guess," he said. He cast one more longing look at the steaming tub and started running. He didn't even bother to follow the trampled path, but just pushed through the grass as fast as he could. He wasn't sure if he could outrun the Saviors, who had been moving at an inhuman speed, but he had to at least try. Michael burst from the grass and ran across the sand, kicking up plumes of dust behind him and leaving the beautiful oasis far behind. He couldn't see the Saviors who were pursuing him, but now he could feel the tremor of their steps beneath his own feet. With each passing minute it grew in intensity, and he knew they were gaining on him.

He had nearly reached the far edge of the valley when he realized that the dunes up ahead were trembling too. He skidded to a stop just as dozens more Saviors crested the dune in front of him and charged. Michael looked over his shoulder and saw the original band of attackers had nearly closed the distance. There was nowhere for him to run.

"Shit," he said. "What the hell am I supposed to do now?"

He looked around frantically for a weapon, but all he could find was a fist-sized rock lodged in the sand. He dug it up and gripped it hard, wondering if he'd even be able to take out one of the fiends with it. He realized, standing there, white-knuckle-gripping that rock, that he was definitely about to die again. No two ways about it.

Don't give in just yet, Michael.

Michael whirled around, looking for the source of the voice, before realizing it was coming from within.

Relax, drop the rock. Let me take care of this one.

"Spirit Man?" Michael said. Then he smiled. "It's been a while."

Oh, I've been here all along, just beneath the surface. Now, what do you say we take care of our little Savior problem?

"I say let's do it. I'm starting to get a little worried here."

The Spirit Man gathered strength deep within him, preparing for battle. Michael felt the Spirit Man extend outward, drawing power from the swirling sky, the setting sun, the iridescent plants once again reappearing in the lengthening shadow of the dunes. The world itself flowed into Spirit Man, energizing him with the limitless power of life and warmth. Sand began to swirl around Michael's feet, just in gentle eddies at first, then faster and faster, forming a vortex of churning sand which encircled him and completely blocked out the world beyond.

Are you familiar with the Shadow Runner?

Michael shook his head, entranced by the whirling sand.

I am you as you are me. Yet we are different. It is the same with the Shadow Runner. We are both him...when we need to be.

The sand vortex began to pulse with all the colors of the visual spectrum, as if each grain refracted a different shade. The brilliance nearly blinded him, but a moment later the colors vanished and the sand fell to the ground, motionless once more. Michael looked down at himself to find that his ratty, sweat-stained clothes were gone. In their place, he wore a royal blue, military-style uniform and a crisp, high-necked tunic. Dozens of living, moving eyes were set into the fine fabric. Some glowed red and orange, while others were bright yellow, deep purple, or shimmering acid green. Brilliant rows of these eyes covered his entire body. They ran up and down his sleeves, grouped in a diamond pattern across his torso, and striped the legs of his trousers.

Black leather holsters were strapped to Michael's thighs, cradling a pair of huge, gleaming revolvers. Black leather munitions belts crisscrossed his chest and back, loaded with all manner of weaponry: daggers, throwing stars, hand grenades, and more. An additional belt circled his waist and held another set of handguns—forty caliber Berettas—plus pouches containing speed loaders for the revolvers and extra clips for the forties.

"Holy shit," Michael said. "I'm strapped."

You'd better believe it, kid.

Michael looked up at the battalion of Saviors who had paused for a moment, puzzled at his transformation. "Come get me, you ugly creatures," he said.

The Saviors stomped their heavy black boots upon the earth, making it tremble and shudder under Michael's feet. They pounded their spears into the earth and brandished their swords, screaming and cursing. Michael stood his ground. Finally, the Saviors charged.

Michael and Spirit Man moved as one, once again sharing the same body and mind. He drew both revolvers from their holsters and began to fire on the horde. His aim was unerring. Each shot sent a spray of blood and brought down another Savior. But they just kept coming. When the revolvers ran out of bullets, he dropped them, drew his Berettas, and whirled around to fire on the Saviors charging from behind him. His shots shattered masks, punctured hearts, and stained the sand dark with blood, but still none of the Saviors so much as flinched. It was as if they fully expected to die, or as if death meant absolutely nothing to them.

They were getting dangerously close now, so Michael pulled the pins out of a couple grenades and lobbed them underhand at the front of the charge on either side. The explosions sent blood, sand, and pieces of bodies raining down, and his ears rang from the blasts.

He almost didn't hear the telltale whistle in time, but managed to sidestep just as a spear tore past. It barely missed him, slicing a bit of his coat sleeve as it passed. The tip lodged into the stomach of a Savior on the other side. Michael ducked as another spear sailed toward his head, and realized the time for guns had passed. Hand to hand combat was his only option now.

Heart pounding, he drew the a pair of daggers and settled into a combat stance. The Saviors might have been a lot bigger than him, but he was nimbler, faster, and, without a doubt, smarter. He wasn't sure what his odds were against the thirty or forty Saviors who remained alive and bloodthirsty, but he felt pretty good about them.

The first Savior reached Michael and swung down at him with a huge broadsword. Michael managed to step out of the way at the last second and retaliated with his daggers, slicing the masked man's jugular clean open. An instant later, two more attackers were on him, lunging with their bare hands. Michael ducked and then thrust upward with both knives, puncturing the Saviors' hearts. Blood ran down his arms, darkening his uniform. He let the bodies fall to his feet and turned to face the rest of his assailants. Piece by piece, he carved them up, dodging and feinting and parrying, then following up with deadly precision. He felt—as he bobbed and weaved and sliced and stabbed—almost like a dancer, so elegant was his performance. Yes, he thought, leaping onto a Savior's back and puncturing his brain stem with one well-placed blow before pushing off and rolling across the sand to avoid a jabbing spear. He was a dancer who brought not joy or wonder to an audience, but clean, beautiful death.

Soon enough, the last Savior fell lifeless at his feet. A wide circle of crimson extended outward from where Michael stood, piled here and there with limp corpses. His uniform was covered in blood. As his breath slowed and the adrenaline left him, he stopped feeling quite so gleeful about his proficiency in inflicting violence. He looked down at his daggers, drenched in blood as they were, and dropped them in disgust. He'd had no choice, of course, but there was something undeniably grotesque about the aftermath of the battle. These dozens of Saviors, insane and bloodthirsty though they may have been, had awoken this morning with life coursing through their veins. Now, as the sun melted into the horizon, they had none. All that was left of them was a red tangle of empty vessels which contained not even an echo of the miraculous thing they had once held.

Michael sighed and started once more toward the edge of the valley when the ground again began to tremble. This time was far worse, however. It felt like an earthquake had seized the valley and was only growing in intensity. Michael looked to the crest of the nearest dune just in time to see not dozens, but hundreds of Saviors pouring over it, waving swords and axes and rifles. Michael re-loaded his guns and picked up his daggers, but looking out across the army charging toward him didn't fill him with much confidence. Sure, he had just dispatched a few dozen of these things with ease, but there were at least ten times that number approaching now, if not twenty. Could he really manage all that?

He braced himself for the fight, vowing to do battle until the bitter end if he had to. But something inside him stayed his hand as he reached for his revolvers.

The Visionaries are few, but we have allies everywhere. We do not need to fight every battle ourselves.

As if on cue, a great rift appeared in the sky, blazing white against the sunset hues. Hundreds of strange shapes began pouring out of the glare. Each was like a great shimmering ball of highly reflec-tive metal. Some were only a foot or so across, while others were much larger, six or even eight feet at their widest. At the edges, they seemed to grow increasingly thinner and less substantial, finally feathering out into the nothingness of air. In their centers, huge eyes glittered, much like the ones on Michael's uniform. They blink-ed and darted back and forth, as if surveying the chaos below them with disdain. They ranged in color from brilliant yellow to emerald green to the deepest glowing purple; some were red, some were electric blue, and some were every color of the rainbow, swirling and pulsing like the skies above them. Like human eyes, each was fringed with thick lashes.

The Saviors paused their charge. They turned to watch the great eyes that hovered over the valley with no small measure of terror. Michael stared too. He had never seen such a thing before.

They are Sight Benders. Ancient allies of the Visionary race.

"What's a Visionary?" Michael said.

You are. We are.

At that, the air crackled with electricity. The Sight Benders, having ascertained the situation, darted toward the crowd of Saviors. To Michael's shock, the Saviors turned tail and began to flee.

Of course, on the open desert, there was nowhere for them to run. The air rippled with smoke as the massive gleaming eyes unleased their power. Sharp bursts of blue and orange flame shot from their pupils, as tightly focused and deadly as laser beams. Entire lines of Saviors collapsed in smoldering, shrieking heaps on the sand. In mere minutes, more than a hundred of the creatures lay smoking on the ground.

The Sight Benders tore through the horde, blowing them apart, tearing off limbs and heads with each sharp blast. The survivors of the initial assault tried to scatter and flee in all directions, but the Sight Benders were quick and nimble in the air and cut off any possible escape. Great plumes of awful-smelling smoke rose from the masses of corpses, and still the blasts kept coming. Michael had to shield his eyes from the staggering brightness of it all.

One particularly brave Savior stopped fleeing and turned his rifle on a Sight Bender, but before he could even pull the trigger a gout of flame incinerated weapon and warrior both. In short order, nothing remained but a few doomed stragglers, dragging their melted, smoking bodies across the sand and leaving a dark trail behind them.

Michael stared at the carnage. He hadn't so much as flexed a muscle or moved so much as an inch, yet his enemies lay dead before him.

"Couldn't they have shown up back in Fort Huachuca?" he said.

The Sight Benders do not experience reality as we do. Sometimes they exist in this world, sometimes they do not. We cannot always count on them for their assistance.

Michael nodded. He didn't entirely understand, but he couldn't argue with the results.

Having finished their work, the Sight Benders gathered near the crest of the dune. They looked at Michael and blinked in unison.

"Thank you," he said. "You just saved my life."

The eyes blinked again, then swiveled and disappeared back into the rift from which they'd come. A moment later, the tear in the sky sealed itself, and all was as it had been before. Peaceful, still, quiet. A cool, evening wind rolled across the desert, carrying ash with it as well as sand.

Chapter 8

Michael stared across the bloody sand, suddenly exhausted. The uniform and weapons of the Shadow Runner drifted away on the wind and Michael was left in his old, dirt-streaked shirt and trousers. He was glad to be left wearing anything, but he still felt uncertain about what he'd just witnessed and participated in. All that death, the massacre in front of him, it was almost more than he could stand.

But the moon was rising, the stars were coming out, and the desert began to shine once again. The path reappeared and urged him along, so he walked, trying not to look at the charred, mangled corpses all around.

As he walked, the rust-red dunes began to change. First they paled to a pinkish color, then finally to pure white. Here and there great sparkling white boulders jutted up from the desert floor, and the iridescent plants were crusted gray-green with a fine coating of pale silt. Michael tripped over something and landed hard. When he turned to see what he'd stumbled on, he saw ancient, rusted railroad tracks which trailed off into the dunes ahead. The shimmering path followed the tracks almost exactly.

"Let's hope these tracks go someplace better than the last set," he said. Then he got up, brushed himself off, and followed them across the vast, glittering white wasteland. As he walked, he couldn't help but dwell on the battle that had just unfolded. Even though Michael knew that the horde would have gleefully ripped him limb from limb, it was still disturbing to have witnessed so much carnage. All the death, the ones who had died at his hands and those who had not. How much weight did all of that carry? Even more disturbing: would the burden grow heavier as the death toll grew— or would it grow lighter? He just hoped that the City of Dreams would be a peaceful place.

The empty quiet of the night allowed Michael to sink deeper into his grim thoughts. He saw the world, his world, engulfed in the sickness that had claimed the badlands. He saw it turn gray and dead, home only to fanatics and fighters who drank themselves into oblivion to forget what had happened to their homes.

Finally, the tracks in the sand stopped abruptly, jarring him from his dark reverie. Michael stared at the spot where the tracks simply ended and puzzled over their purpose. Tracks from nowhere when went nowhere. And not a train to be seen. What kind of planning was that? He kept walking and reached a bank where the sand sloped sharply downwards. Beyond, the land became impossibly flat. A cracked, lifeless expanse stretching off into infinity. Nothing glimmered here. No colorful plants poked up from the cracks. Michael soon understood what he was looking at. Salt flats. The remains of an ancient sea which had long ago dried up, leaving behind only its salt which kept anything from growing here. A truly desolate place.

Despite the lack of a shimmering path, Michael still sensed the route he was destined to follow, and it led across these seemingly endless flats. Better to cross them at night, at least. There was no telling how vast they were, and he knew how quickly heat and dehydration could kill you in a place like this. He walked out onto the flats, his footfalls eerily loud in the silent night. He walked until he could no longer see the shore he had left from, then kept walking across that great emptiness. Finally, he noticed something different on the far horizon. Something which broke the monotonous flatness of the seabed. As he approached, it grew larger, eventually revealing itself to be a perfect circle of huge stone spires jutting skyward, surrounding a monolithic block of sandstone that was far too perfectly shaped to be natural. Michael stepped into the circle, then stopped. His own breathing was the only sound in the world, but he had the peculiar sensation that something was about to happen. Judging by recent experience, he guessed it wasn't going to be something good.

The monolith bore two words, engraved deep in the stone with elegant letters: Suck Fly.

He traced the letters' curving arcs with a fingertip, but had to admit he had no idea what it meant. Did it refer to something, or someone? And if so, where were they? He looked again around the circle of spires and saw no one, yet still he felt a deep unease in his heart. A hot wind flowed between the stones, wafting clouds of salt into the air, and on that wind he caught a whiff of death.

He had been here before, he was almost certain of it. The memory was buried under too much sand to recall clearly, but he saw three figures with him—a woman and two children, each around eleven or twelve. They were familiar, yet strangers at the same time. The woman's eyes told him she knew him, but perhaps he did not know her. A name danced on the tip of his tongue but would not reveal itself. Then the memory retreated back beneath the sand and Michael was entirely alone once again.

Michael scrubbed a hand over his dusty forehead and sighed. "Just once, I wish I understood what the hell was going on around here," he said.

Just then, from afar, he heard a slight disruption in the air. He strained his ears and gradually, as the sound grew nearer, discerned the slow beating of an immense pair of wings.

<h1 style="text-align:center">Chapter 9</h1>

In the distant sky, a black spot appeared and began to grow. Michael focused on the dot with his newly improved vision and didn't like what he saw. It looked almost like a massive, diseased vulture whose feathers had been falling out. Only a few black plumes still clung to its bony, batlike wings. His eyes caught on the talons next, each nearly as long as he was tall and already stained with old, dry blood. Most striking, however, was the creature's head. Instead of a vulture's head, there was a woman's torso and head, the former coated in red feathers and the latter seething with yellow-eyed rage. Tangled white hair dangled across her face, which was twisted into a snarl. Her arms were thick and muscular and ringed with bracelets of bone. Michael ascertained pretty quickly that this creature was not likely to be a friend. But, looking across the salt flats, he also realized running would be pointless. Better to stay here, where at least the rock spires could offer some sort of cover if he needed it.

The beast closed the distance with remarkable speed. As she neared, the beating of her enormous wings stirred up clouds of dust and salt which swept across the plain. Michael had to shield his eyes to avoid being blinded. With a final push through the air, the creature soared over his head and landed with a crash atop the rectangular stone. *Ah,* Michael thought. *This must be Suck Fly, then.*

She flapped her wings softly, then tucked them by her sides and glared down at him.

"Spirit Man," she rasped. "What an unexpected little treat."

"I have nothing for you," he said. "I don't want any trouble."

She laughed and flapped her wings for emphasis, blowing another cloud of dust into the air. "Naïve little Spirit Man, you have exactly what I need."

"And what's that?"

She laughed again, noticeably less amused this time. "Your voice."

Well, that wasn't good. Michael tried to dip into the well inside of himself from which the Shadow Runner had emerged before, but it was bone dry. He got the sense the form needed recovery time between appearances, which wasn't great for his current predicament. All he could really do was stall.

"Since it's my voice and all," he said, "would you mind telling me what you plan to use it for?"

Suck Fly leaned toward him and smiled, exposing a mouth full of blackened, rotting teeth and pus-oozing gums. "Your vision quest is over," she said. "Look around you. Have you seen anything worth saving since returning to Shook? It's a land of death, misery, and hardship. A land parched and desolate. What difference does it make if the sickness of the badlands consumes the whole damn place?"

"You're blind," Michael said. "Shook isn't desolate—not even the dunes beyond this seabed. It's full of life like anywhere else. I won't let you or the Saviors or anyone else destroy that."

"My, my, aren't you the little do-gooder. But Spirit Man, I hope you understand I was only trying to help you. The sooner you learn to let go of this world, the easier it will be to watch it be destroyed."

Michael again reached inside of himself, seeking the power he needed, and again didn't find what he was looking for. This time, however, he sensed something else, something that wasn't the Shadow Runner but which could still help him fight. He prodded it with his mind, curious about this new arrival.

Then he felt the voice of Spirit Man within.

I see you have uncovered the Blade Master. And not a moment too soon.

Michael looked up at Suck Fly. "All right then," he said. "Enough screwing around, let's get this over with."

Adrenaline surged through his veins. As he touched the new form for the first time, its power reverberated through him with such intensity that he felt like he was about to fly apart. Then a massive surge of energy exploded up from first one rocky spire, then another, then another, until the whole circle was emitting crackling blue-green beams into the night sky. The beams coalesced into a shimmering oval which then descended and engulfed Michael. He spread his arms and let the energy wrap around him, transforming him into something new. The sound of bending, folding metal filled the air as his body was enfolded by a sheet of armor. Thin, flexible and lightweight metal soon covered Michael from head to toe, but he knew that for all its flexibility, it was incredibly durable; nothing in any world, dream or otherwise, could withstand punishment like this metal. Like so many things in this strange world, the armor was many different colors. The face mask was an iridescent gold, shimmering under the moonlight and shifting through shades of blue, green, yellow and purple with every move that the Spirit Man made. The breast plate and leg guards were mostly black and orange, accented with iridescent discs set in a diamond pattern. Two longswords appeared in his hands, expertly crafted from the same metal as his armor.

Suck Fly shrieked in anger at the transformation. "Tricky tricky Spirit Man," she said. "That tin can won't be enough to save you." Then she dove at him with her talons outstretched.

Michael, unhindered by his lightweight armor, leapt out of the way and swung his swords in an arc behind him as he moved. He slashed Suck Fly's leg as she swept by and black blood spattered the ground. She screamed, beat her wings, and ascended out of his reach before whirling on him again. She darted toward him again, but this time feinted left before pivoting right at the last second. Michael didn't have time to dodge. The huge talons wrapped around his torso and wrenched him into the air. Suck Fly cackled and squeezed tighter, forcing the air out of his lungs. Then she swung past one of the rock spires and smashed him against it.

Pain shot through Michael's shoulder and he dropped one of his swords. He watched it tumble to the cracked earth below and growled. With a burst of strength, he wrenched his other arm free

    VISION OF THE SPIRIT MAN

of the talons and slashed at Suck Fly's vulture leg over and over again. She shrieked again and released him.

Michael plummeted thirty feet and landed hard. He groaned, then rolled over and struggled to his hands and knees. There, not twenty paces ahead of him, was his other sword. If he could just get to it before Suck Fly reached him...

He started crawling, wincing at the pain that tore through him with every movement. He had definitely broken something, or at least badly bruised just about everything. The armor might have been nearly impervious to Suck Fly's slicing talons, but it sure didn't help much against a fall. When he was halfway to the sword, he heard flapping wings behind him. Suck Fly had regained her composure and was preparing for another attack. Michael picked up the pace as much as he could, struggling across the salty earth one painful movement at a time. He heard the rush of air approaching as Suck Fly dove, and he leapt forward, snatched up his second sword, and rolled onto his back. He swung hard and black blood spattered all over his armor. Two of Suck Fly's talons dropped to the ground, severed from their owner. Michael stood and faced his wounded opponent.

Suck Fly, incensed and in agony, let loose a litany of curses at him, most of which he'd never even heard before but understood by the venom in her tone. Then she began to beat her wings straight down, not moving in the sky but kicking up tremendous amounts of dust around Michael. She flapped harder, and soon formed a miniature dust storm inside the circle of stone spires. Michael tried to shield his eyes but the dust whipped at him all the same. He couldn't see more than a few inches in front of his face, and started finding it hard to breathe.

He didn't see Suck Fly approaching until she materialized through the storm a foot away and crashed into him, sending him sprawling back against a stone spire. The back of his head hit the stone hard and for a few moments all he saw were multicolored blots appearing and disappearing in front of him. Michael pulled off his helmet and threw it aside. When he put his fingertips to the back of his head, they came away dark with blood.

"Shit," he said.

As the dust around him settled, he spotted Suck Fly once more perched atop the stone that bore her name. She had wrapped her wings around her like a cape and was watching him warily. Blood from her mutilated leg seeped down the face of the stone.

"Have you had enough yet, Spirit Man?" she said. "We don't have to keep dragging this out. Just lay down your swords and come with me. I promise I'll be gentle. At least, mostly gentle."

He spat out blood and realized he must have bitten his tongue when he hit his head. His ears were ringing and he felt dazed, like everything was moving in slow motion and just a little bit blurry.

"What," he said, "you aren't having fun? I'm having a blast."

He tried to assume his usual combat stance but couldn't hide how injured he was. It was obvious in the slowness of his movements, the way he flinched when he moved a particular joint this way or that. Suck Fly noticed immediately. She chuckled.

"Look at you. You're finished. Just admit you're done and surrender."

Why wasn't she just finishing him off? He knew she could if she wanted to, so what was holding her back? Something about this wasn't adding up, and he didn't like it. There was some motive behind those predatory yellow eyes that made this creature far, far more dangerous than the savage Saviors who seemed content to kill and burn without any thought beyond the immediate moment of battle.

"What are you waiting for?" Michael said. "Are you afraid of me?"

At this, Suck Fly let loose a tremendous laugh and spread her wings wide. Michael saw his chance and didn't hesitate. He wound up and hurled one of his swords directly at the horrid thing atop the pedestal. It sailed through the air—a perfect throw. Suck Fly had only an instant to recognize what was happening and her eyes went wide. But there was nothing she could do. The sword pierced her heart, driving deep into the feathers and burying itself all the way up to its hilt. She let out a strangled cry and tried to pull it out,

     VISION OF THE SPIRIT MAN

but her strength was quickly leaving her. Black blood spewed from the wound and completely covered the engraved name on the rock. Suck Fly tried to speak but only managed a gurgle as blood spilled from her lips. Then she reached toward Michael as if promising revenge, tottered back and forth a little, and tumbled headlong off her perch. She landed on the ground with a tremendous crash, lifeless.

Michael breathed a long sigh of relief, though even something as simple as breathing sent sharp pains through his chest. He longed for the mysterious oasis bathtub and its strange healing powers. Cautious at first, but growing bolder once he realized she would not be moving again, Michael walked around the crooked body of Suck Fly. He had never before encountered something like this, something so powerful and deadly.

"I just hope there aren't more of you," he said, though he knew already that this hope was in vain. Spirit Man's voice within him confirmed this.

She is one of the gods of the dream world, but she is not the only one. Be wary of them, Michael Seymour. They are stronger than even I.

"Is she...dead? Like, dead dead?"

Oh, come now. You know better than that. Gods do not die here, just as we do not.

Michael was about to ask another question when something peculiar started happening to the bird-woman's body. Gradually at first, then with accelerating speed, it began to turn gray, like stone or ash. The transformation started at the edges and worked its way inward until the entire corpse was the color of slate. Then a particularly strong wind rushed through the circle of stones and the body dissolved into it—just ash scattering across the desert on the wind.

Slowly, the glimmering armor and fierce weapons of the Blade Master began to fade. When they finally disappeared entirely, Michael stood, wobbling a little, dressed as before in his tattered slacks and dress shirt in front of the bloody stone pedestal. He fell to his knees and dry heaved as the Blade Master's inhuman energy vanished from him, leaving his body so sore and exhausted, he could barely move. After taking some time to recover, he struggled to his feet, unsure if he would be able to do that again anytime soon.

When Michael turned to continue following his invisible path, he was surprised to see a tiny Sight Bender—the smallest he had ever seen. It was only about two inches wide. Incredibly, two tiny white butterflies fluttered in the depths of its little blue-green iris. A long string hung off one edge of it, so that it resembled a little kite decorated with a floating eyeball. It hovered there, staring at him, as if trying to communicate some kind of message it was not able to convey in words he would understand.

Michael reached out to touch the white string but the little Sight Bender flitted away, up into the air and just beyond his reach. Then it dove back down toward him, only to zip away the moment his hand drew near. Up, down, away, and then back to him; it did this several times, until Michael finally figured out what it wanted him to do. Each time the little Sight Bender moved forward, Michael followed it—just a step or two at first, but soon Michael was walk-ing very briskly, following the amazing creature out of the small clearing and onto the salt flats.

As Michael walked, he felt powerful tremors rumbling deep within the earth beneath his feet. He looked back to see the stone spires and the pedestal marked with Suck Fly's name collapse to the earth, sending plumes of debris in every direction. A few pebble-sized fragments bounced across the plain and landed at his feet. He picked one up, put it in his pocket, and kept moving, just following the eye in the sky. The two of them traveled across the salt bed for hours upon hours. The sun rose, the heat grew almost unbearable, then the sun began to set again. Still they journeyed on. Sometimes the eye would float down toward him, tempting him to reach for its long white string, but whenever Michael leapt up to try and grab the string, the eye would zip back up into the sky.

Finally, as the sun slipped across the horizon in the western sky,

Michael came upon another strange sight. Out there in the middle of nowhere, with not another soul to be seen, stood a huge picnic table, shaded by a big green awning and laid with all kinds of food and drink. Michael was famished. It had been so long since he'd eaten anything, he was actually surprised that he could still walk, much less fight. There were plates of fruit and bread, chunks of roasted pork and beef, fried chicken, salad greens, cheeses and nuts, and even a huge chocolate cake. Better yet, everything looked perfectly fresh, as if it had been set out for him mere moments before he had arrived. Nearby, a semi-familiar sign jutted from the dry earth which read: *Eat, traveler.* Again, he was suspicious at first, but he figured that the well had turned out just fine after all, so he could probably trust this mysterious picnic too. So he ate and drank until his stomach was full and his heart was content. As he did so, the eye hovered nearby, just out of his reach, floating serenely in the sky above him.

When he was so full he couldn't swallow another bite, he lay down on the bench where he had been sitting. The moon rose slowly, and a cool breeze blew across the sands. Michael considered how many days he had been walking for without rest, and couldn't believe it had taken him this long to let himself sleep. He still had no idea where he was, of course, but if he was honest with himself, he was starting to think that didn't really matter anymore. No matter where he was, his objective was fairly straightforward: just keep going.

"I'm always lost," he said. "Lost in this unbelievable dream world. Lost back home in the real world. Lost in between the two and in both at once. All in all, it's not so bad."

Sighing, Michael closed his eyes and pushed his troubled thoughts aside. In minutes, he was fast asleep, and following his dreams like a long winding river emptying into the sea.

Chapter 10

Michael wandered through the desert for a long, long time, following the little Sight Bender, which would occasionally turn around as if to make sure he was keeping pace. They left the salt flats behind and found themselves again among the dunes. Michael couldn't help but wonder if he had somehow walked in just a big circle and ended up right back where he started. All the dunes looked familiar, and he could have sworn he had seen each and every one of them before. His worries vanished, however, when they crested a dune and he spotted something that was definitely new. Up ahead was a cracked, paved road winding through the desert, and on that road he saw a green army tank. It sat parked in the middle of a crumbling strip of asphalt, utterly out of place but seemingly unaware of how much it did not belong. Vultures circled over the tank. Gunshots rang out across the sand.

Michael dove to the ground but soon realized the shots weren't directed at him. Feeling a little foolish, he stood, brushed himself off, and squinted in the direction of the tank. He had to blink hard and look again before he believed what he was seeing. Crouched alongside the metal behemoth were a woman and two kids—the very same ones he had seen in his vision at the stone spires. The woman held an assault rifle and each kid brandished a pistol. Every few seconds, they peered over the tank treads and fired a few shots before ducking back down. Looking past the tank, Michael spotted a group of charging Saviors, each carrying guns of their own and returning fire. Bullets pinged off the tank just as the woman ducked behind it, missing her head by mere inches. Without hesitation, Michael raced to join the fray.

Only once he took cover behind the tank with the scrappy trio did he realize his fighting forms had not yet replenished. He would have to figure out how to manage this battle as plain old Michael Seymour. No swords, no daggers, no grenades.

As soon as he dove behind the tank, the woman whirled on him and he found himself staring directly down the barrel of her assault rifle.

"Whoa, whoa," he said. "I'm one of the good guys."

The kids backed away, keeping their pistols trained on him, but she smirked and lowered her gun.

"Spirit Man," she said. "Long time."

Before he could respond, a burst of gunshots tore through the air and everyone ducked down further.

"Here," the woman said. She pulled a pistol from her belt and handed it to him. "We'll catch up in a second."

Michael peeked over the tank and a bullet whistled past his ear. He ducked back down.

"Did you piss them off or something?" he said. "They seem pretty upset."

The woman fired three quick bursts, taking down a few of the attackers. "Oh, probably," she said. "Might have something to do with how we stole their tank."

Michael leaned to the side and fired off a few shots, striking one Savior in the chest and one in the head. Both collapsed but, as usual, their compatriots charge on, unfazed. At first, it looked like the fight was almost over. There were maybe a half dozen Saviors left standing and one or two more wounded on the ground, still trying to crawl forward or fire their weapons. But just as Michael made this observation, he heard something approaching from the distance, something like a deep mechanical roar. Were those... car engines? He peeked out over the dunes and saw, far off but rapidly closing in, a long line of dune buggies tearing toward them. The vehicles kicked up an immense wall of dust behind them that made it appear as if they were bringing a sandstorm with them. Each buggy had a fifty caliber machine gun atop it, manned by Saviors.

"Uh, guys?" Michael said.

"Yeah, I see it," the woman said as she let loose another burst of rounds. "We should think about getting out of here."

"*Think* about it?" one of the kids, the girl, said.

"Okay, okay, we *will* get out of here, just give me one…second…" She fired one more shot directly between the last charging Savior's eyes. "Okay, now we can go. Hop in!" She scrambled atop the tank and, with a grunt, heaved open the metal hatch. The kids clambered after her and dropped inside. She shot Michael a look. "Well? What are you waiting for?"

She offered her hand, helped pull him onto the tank, and dropped through the hatch. He followed her just as one of the buggies opened fire, and he slammed the hatch shut behind him. The tank was much smaller inside than Michael had expected. With the four of them in there together, it was positively claustrophobic. Thick metal walls pressed in on all sides, bedecked in all sorts of instruments he couldn't identify. The woman set herself up in the pilot's seat and started flipping switches.

"You know how to drive this thing?" Michael said.

"More or less. You know how to operate the gun?"

"I'm sure I can figure it out."

"Well, hop to it. The armor won't hold up against those guns forever."

As if on cue, a string of rounds pounded the right side of the tank, strafing it from front to back. The armor held but, judging by the small dents which appeared on the inside, it would be best not to test how strong that armor really was. Michael raced to the gun controls and tried to figure out how the hell to operate them. He stared at the display, the throttle-like stick, the various measurements with dismay, unable to decipher it. Then he felt a gentle tap on his arm. The boy, about ten or eleven years old, flipped a couple switches and the display came to life.

"Use this," he said, pointing to the stick, which Michael now saw had a trigger on it.

"Uh, thanks," Michael said. Then he sat down and got to work. Through the display, he could see the fast-approaching dune buggies and a green aiming reticule projected over them. He turned the gun and pulled the trigger. An explosion rocked the dunes, sending buckets of sand raining down. When it cleared, he saw he had missed his target. He tried again and this time the dune buggy exploded, shards of metal flying everywhere as the two Saviors on board were vaporized in the blast. The rest were just about in firing range. He looked over his shoulder.

"We aren't we moving yet? Is everything okay?"

"Yeah, yeah," the woman said. "Like I said, 'more or less.'"

Suddenly, the tank lurched forward and began to move with surprising speed across the desert. The kids cheered and high fived each other.

"See? Told you I could do it."

Michael chuckled and returned to the task at hand. The movement of the tank, rolling and bumping along, traversing rises and dips on the road, made his job of aiming a whole lot harder, but he did what he could. He let loose one shell, then another, then another, blasting a few more buggies to pieces. He blew half the wheels off of one, sending it careening into its closest neighbor and turning both vehicles into a tangled heap of scrap. The Saviors who had been thrown from their rides on collision struggled to their feet and started sprinting across the sand, but quickly disappeared inside the dust cloud kicked up by their allies.

When the buggies got close enough, they split into two columns. One went right, one went left, flanking the tank. They opened fire at the same time, riddling the armor with bullets. Unlike before, they didn't have to fire in bursts anymore, and just kept shooting as belts of ammunition snaked from boxes on the floor of their vehicles. The shots rattled against the tank with increasing volume, and the dents they created kept getting larger, but Michael tried to keep his cool. He had to take out one side first, then switch to the other—the gun pivoted too slowly to do it any other way. He took aim at the closest attacker and blew them to pieces.

"How are we doing back there?" the woman shouted. He could barely hear her over the sound of bullets crashing into the tank.

"I'm doing my best," he said. He fired again and took out another, but the rain of bullets wouldn't let up. Any minute now they'd start to break through.

"I'm gonna try something," the pilot said.

"What?"

"I said I'm gonna try something!"

"No, I meant, what are you—"

Before he could finish his sentence, the tank lurched violently and the woman veered hard to the right. Had it not been for their masks, Michael was sure he would have seen expressions of shock and horror in the second the Saviors had to process what was happening. Then the tank smashed into their line of buggies, flipping them, snapping their axels, and even crushing one beneath its treads.

"Hot damn!" Michael said.

"Don't thank me, just finish the ones on your side."

He did. A few more pulls of the trigger, a few more shells, and all that was left of the marauding Saviors was a lot of rubble and a whole lot of smoke. The tank rolled to a stop and for a moment the group sat in silence.

"So," Michael said.

"So," said the woman. "You don't remember us, do you?"

"I think I do. A little bit." Michael strained to remember. "It's all bits and pieces, but we've known each other for a long time, haven't we?"

She nodded. "And my name?"

He reached deep into his unconscious, grasping for the word which seemed always just beyond the reach of his fingers. Finally, he grabbed it.

"Trip," he said.

She smiled. "So you remember something. And these are Noel and Nevaeh." She gestured to the boy and the girl. They waved enthusiastically. "We've fought side by side with you more times than I can count. I'm glad to see you haven't lost your touch for it."

"Why can't I remember any of this?" Michael said.

Trip suddenly looked quite sad. "Well," she said, "each time you die, you forget things. You forget people."

"How could I forget you?"

She shrugged. "Easily."

Feeling a little ashamed and eager to change the subject, Michael said, "So do you know what the hell is going on in this place? Who are the Saviors and what's their problem with us? And who the hell is Annihilator? And what's the deal with the wall? And who's leading the Saviors?"

"Whoa, slow down there, mister—you've got an awful lot of questions, apparently, and I'm gonna be honest, I probably can't answer most of them. I may not be new to the dream world, but all this badlands stuff sure is new to me. To be honest, I'm still trying to sort it all out myself."

Michael nodded. It wasn't the answer he'd hoped for, but he couldn't blame her. Especially not given the fact that he barely seemed able to remember anything about his previous adventures in this strange realm.

"What I do know," Trip said, "is that sometimes there's no reason for anything here, no explanation. And if you do manage to get an explanation? It usually makes no sense at all."

"Yeah, I get that feeling. A captain wrote me a note that was supposed to explain everything, but it just left me with more questions than I had before I read it."

"So?" Noel piped up. "Things that make sense are overrated."

"Mmm hmm!" his sister agreed.

Michael dislodged himself from the gunner's seat and knelt beside the kids.

"You two must have a pretty unique way of looking at the world, having spent so much time here growing up."

"Not as unique as you," Nevaeh said. When he frowned, she pointed to his eyes. "You can look at stuff in a much weirder way."

"How did you...?"

Trip shook her head. "They just know things. Perceptive little rascals. They pick up on stuff real fast, even stuff I'd never catch in a thousand years."

"Can you use your special eyes on me?" Noel said.

"Well," said Michael, "I don't know. Let's see."

He concentrated, not expecting to see anything of note, but gasped when the orb's vision kicked in.

"What?" Trip said. "What do you see?" She sounded a little panicked by his shocked reaction.

"I see…" Michael trailed off, struggling to put what he saw into words. A million tiny beads of light swirled around Noel and Nevaeh like electrons around an atom, tracing brilliant comet trails through the air. When he held out his hand to touch one, they shifted ever-so-slightly, so as to be always just outside his grasp. But he sensed that there was much more than light contained within these flitting things. They radiated something else, something like…possibility. That was it. Each tiny particle contained a possible life these children could live, possible paths they could follow, worlds they could inhabit, people they could meet or not meet, enemies they could make or avoid, stories they could accrue over the course of lives that were long or short or somewhere in between. Michael had never seen anything like it. All those unrealized worlds circling, circling, waiting for their turn to become reality. He couldn't quite peer into them, couldn't see specifics, but he felt the weight of potential contained within each. These children were bathed in the light of the future.

"I see how bright they really are," Michael said. "Your children are magnificent."

"Thanks, but we already know that," Nevaeh said.

Michael blinked and the shining futures went away. The inside of the tank was once again dim, lit only by computer screens, and existed only in the present. He felt a strange sort of loss at the disappearance of the little electrons, as if with their vanishing he had lost access to infinite futures and settled, once more, into a single linear path. He felt the tug of that path still, urging him onward to the City of Dreams, whatever that was. He looked at Trip, suddenly certain of what he needed to ask her.

"Trip. Who are the Visionaries?"

She laughed. "Funny question, coming from one."

"No, I know that, but...what does it mean for me to be one?"

"Well, for starters," she said, "it makes you like us. We're Visionaries too. Some of the last. In fact, if this tank were to suddenly blow up and take all of us out, that would eliminate a pretty significant percentage of the world's remaining Visionaries."

Michael smiled uneasily and looked at the weapons panel to make sure nothing was armed and likely to fire backwards into the tank.

"It also means," Trip continued, "that we have a lot of enemies, just for being who we are. The Saviors, for one, but the list is long and certainly doesn't end there."

"What other enemies do we have?"

"Well, demons, for one. Bat demons in particular."

"Bat demons?"

"Yep, just as mean and nasty as you'd imagine them, based on the name. See, our people have been at war with the demons and their generals for essentially forever. The fighting might have a beginning, long lost to history, but it sure as hell doesn't have an end. Over time, they've killed a lot more of us than we have of them. And I mean permanently—dead dead, none of this waking up in a daze somewhere. They've found methods to just... step foot into the dream world, you've got an automatic target on your back. Does that about answer your question?"

"Well, it definitely explains a whole lot of things. And the Saviors are working together with these demons?"

Trip shrugged. "I'd call it an uneasy truce. Both of 'em want to tear down the wall around the badlands, so they're working together for now—more or less."

Michael nodded. It felt good to receive the first real answers since his arrival in all this chaos, even if he didn't necessarily like the information Trip gave him. When did he ask to be part of some generations-long war, anyway? Didn't he get a say in all this?

Trip peered at the various displays by the pilot's seat. "Still no movement out there," she said. "Shall we continue on?"

"No use dawdling," Michael said. "Onward."

<h1 style="text-align:center">Chapter 11</h1>

If there was one major problem with rolling across the desert in a heavily armored tank, it was the heat. The machine had air conditioning, but it didn't do much good against the withering rays of the sun. Michael wiped his dripping brow.

"I feel like we're boiling alive in here," he said.

"More like steaming," Noel said.

"Well," Trip added, "we are sitting in a giant metal can. But, point taken. We should probably look for some real shelter, shouldn't we?"

Michael nodded. "That would be grand." He drained the last of a canteen Trip had given him and looked around for more. No luck. The tank trundled on.

Finally, just when Michael thought he couldn't make it another minute in that sweltering space, Trip shouted and pointed excitedly.

"Rocks up ahead. Looks like a perfect place to catch some shade."

A moment later, she ground the tank to a halt.

"Okay, folks, let's get the hell out of here."

Michael opened the hatch and all of them climbed out, grateful for the fresh air despite the fact that it was, if anything, even hotter outside. Michael stood atop the tank and had to close his eyes against the blinding light—so bright after spending so long in the tank's dim interior. After a long minute during which he thought he might never be able to see again, his eyes finally adjusted enough to peer around beneath the shade of his fingers.

Just beside the tank stood a large pile of boulders. It was as if a giant had sat there playing, stacking pebbles on top of each other to see how tall his pile would get before it fell over. The prospect of shade was so exciting that Michael began to scramble down the tank without thinking. He pressed his hand against the metal to lower himself down, cried out in pain as the sunbaked armor burned him, and tumbled the rest of the way to the ground, landing in a cloud of dust and coughing as he breathed it in. The kids laughed hysterically at this, and after a moment Trip appeared by his side.

"Oh, I should mention," she said. "The tank can get a little hot when it's been in the sun. You should be careful about that."

Michael offered a halfhearted thumbs up. "Noted. Thank you oh so much."

"You're fine. Now let's go get some shade, you big dummy."

Trip helped him to his feet and they made their way to the stone pile. The sun was almost directly overhead, so the pile cast little shade in any direction, but Michael noticed something as the group circled it, searching for the best spot to cool off.

"Hold on," he said. He poked at one of the rocks.

"Something wrong?" Trip said. Her hand was already on the holster of her pistol, ready to protect her kids from whatever Michael was seeing.

"Nothing like that," he said. He pulled away one of the smaller stones to reveal a gap, then removed a few more to reveal a tunnel. "Come on, give me a hand with this."

A few minutes later, the two of them had cleared enough of the rocks to open up the entrance to a tunnel which burrowed under the boulder pile and disappeared into darkness. It wasn't much more than a gap between two of the larger boulders, but, given their current predicament, it couldn't have possibly been more inviting.

"Well, let's go, kids," Michael said. Then he got on all fours and crawled inside. The desert wind was cut short as he entered the dark, dank space. Once again, his eyes had to adjust, this time to the dark. After ten feet or so, he emerged into a large cavern which must have been at the very center of the boulder pile. A shallow basin full of fresh water sat in the center of the cavern.

Noel and Nevaeh ran toward the basin.

"Hang on, kids," Trip said. "Don't stick your grubby mitts in there. We need that water to drink." She took the canteen from Michael, unscrewed the cap, and filled it carefully, along with the others. Everyone drank their fill, and then she refilled the containers.

"Hold out your hands," she instructed, and poured water over the kids' hands and Michael's before washing her own. Then she poured a little more water onto a bandana and used it to wipe the worst of the dust and soot off the kids' faces.

"What do you say we call it a day here and rest up for tomorrow?" Michael said.

"I'm all for it," said Trip. She removed her pack and dug around for a moment before producing some beef jerky and dried apple slices. "It's not much, but it should hold us over for a while." She passed out most of the rations to the eager kids and handed half of what was left to Michael.

"How long have you all been out here?" Michael said. "Living on nothing but this?"

Trip shrugged. "Who can keep track of the days in a place like this? I'm just grateful we haven't run out yet, although, I'll be honest, that day is coming a lot sooner than I'd like it to."

"Are we gonna run out of food?" Noel said. Nevaeh punched him in the arm as if to remind him they weren't supposed to talk about things like that.

"No, sweetie," Trip said. "We'll find more. We always do. And be-sides, now we've got a pretty cool helper in case we get into any more trouble, right?"

Nevaeh giggled. "Well, I wouldn't say *cool*, but he's all right."

Trip smiled at Michael. "We're happy to have you around."

"I'm just glad I found you when I did," Michael said. "Things looked pretty dicey for you and, to be frank, things were pretty dicey for me too at that point."

"That's the funny thing about this place. For all the terrible, horri-fying stuff that happens here, everything always seems to happen in exactly the way it should. Like there's some path we're all sup-posed to follow, even if we don't know it, and if we stray from it for too long, we'll just be nudged back onto it without even realizing."

"You don't find that scary?" Michael said. "Always knowing that there's someplace you *should* be, something you *should* be doing?"

Trip pondered for a moment, then said, "And is that really any different from life outside the dream world?"

"Huh. I guess not."

"So what's there to be afraid of?"

After that, the little tribe ate in companionable silence, gnawing on chewy jerky and apple slices and washing it all down with plenty of water. Finally, their bellies at least somewhat full, the kids curled around each other on the sandy floor and fell asleep. Trip lay down near them and soon she was sleeping too. Michael leaned up against a great, smooth stone and stretched his legs out in front of him. He listened to the slow burble of the spring feeding water into the basin, and marveled at how they had been able to find this place amid the seemingly endless wastes of the desert. Maybe it had been luck, maybe it had been whatever force ensured Michael ran into Trip and Noel and Nevaeh during their battle with the Saviors. Whatever the case, it didn't seem worth it to dwell. They were here, they were safe, and the killing sun was, for now at least, kept at bay. In minutes, Michael too was fast asleep.

Hours later, a horrible, moaning wind jerked Michael from his dreams. Outside, sand whipped at the boulders that formed their meager shelter. Gusts blasted through the cracks between the stones, shrieking and wailing within the narrow passages.

Trip sat up and scrambled for her flashlight. Clicking it on, she looked over at Michael and whispered, "What the hell?"

"Wind," he answered, keeping his voice low. It did no good—both Noel and Nevaeh were already sitting up and looking around, confusion and fear in their sleepy eyes.

"It's okay, kids. It's just the wind," he said reassuringly.

Just then, beyond the entrance, a weird, silvery-white light appeared and grew. Michael got to his feet, one hand on the pistol in his belt.

"Come out, Spirit Man," a terrible growling voice sounded, echoing through the half-darkness inside the cavern. Not the wind, then.

"Who's there?" Michael shouted.

"You know me, Spirit Man. I am the ghost of the Forsaken Ones."

Michael crept toward the entrance of the cave and slowly drew his pistol as he did so. He made sure the safety was off. Trip and the kids followed just behind him, brandishing weapons of their own.

"Come out with your band of lost souls!" screamed the voice.

Weapons ready, the four crept out of the cave and stood before the ghost, staring in awe at his shimmering form. He seemed to be made of both light and mist; each gust of howling wind caused his form to shift and swirl, so that in one moment he was barely present and in the next he was terrifyingly real.

"What do you want?" Michael said.

The ghost floated a few feet above the sand, wearing the tattered, ancient garb of a warrior: leather pants and a roughly woven tunic. A huge shield was strapped to his back, and a broadsword hung from a scabbard at his hip. A brass battle helmet sat snug upon his bald head, and his face was drawn in a rictus of hatred and agony. He leveled a long rifle right at Michael's head.

"Do not try to flee," he said. "Hear what I have to say, or perish."

The ghost was rail thin, hardly more than bones and even those were incorporeal. From his height, however, he might have been a powerful warrior at one time. Michael couldn't help but ask himself what ancient secrets must linger behind that deathly, wizened face.

The ghost gnashed his jagged yellow teeth and howled.

"When the whip comes down, Spirit Man, hellfire will rain down upon the land and catch your hair ablaze! As you can see, I have no hair on my bony skull—nothing to lose, and nothing to fear, for I am long since forsaken by everyone I once held dear!" The ghost sank lower and pointed his long, bony finger at Michael's chest. "Are you afraid of your ghosts, Spirit Man?"

Michael didn't answer. The ghost rambled on.

"This bag of bones has seen long days and dark nights, wandering these lands, alone and forsaken, for a long, long time. For over seven hundred years, I've been trapped in this place, ever since that fateful day when my legions betrayed me, when my friends abandoned me, and left me on the field of battle alone. I watched as the wooden stakes and crosses of death that rose out of the earth to mark my comrades' graves rotted and crumbled into nothingness.

"In the long days and dark nights of my life, my flesh felt much pleasure, but for every instant of joy, I endured ten times as much pain. I thought I would get a reprieve in death. Once my bones and flesh were draped across a wooden cross, bound with chains to rot in the sun and wind. But it was not to be."

Michael glanced over at Trip; she just shrugged and shot him a look that said, "I'm as confused as you are." The kids peeked out from behind her, their eyes still wide at the sight of the ghost's wavering features. And still the ancient spirit rambled on.

"You see, Spirit Man, you and I are alike in many ways. We both seek peace, but all we find is war and fighting and blood, staining the earth all around our feet. We are warriors by birth, and inescapably so. Our paths are fixed and cannot be altered. We walk upon a bloody earth and we drink from rivers flowing with blood. We are a very thirsty lot so we kneel down by the river's edge and drink until we are content. We have long since learned not to flinch at the salty taste of blood on our tongues." The ghost howled in anguish and the wind rose in sympathy, kicking up sand into Michael's eyes.

Suddenly, the ghost swooped down, looming right in front of Michael and Trip, so close that they could almost smell the ancient stench of his breath. "But even as we drink, we still thirst for more blood—there is never enough blood to quench the violence in us. The rivers flow with the innocent blood of everyone who ever lived and ever died. Nobody asked for this world to be the way it is—full of pain and deep sorrow—but it is what it is: terrible and harsh, full of troubles. My eyes are sunken and dark now, blinded by long years, but in my mind's eye I watched the rivers flow into the sea, filling it up with fresh blood."

The ghost paused and seemed to stare off into space, as though contemplating something of great consequence. When he spoke again, his voice was low and melancholy.

"As rivers flow into the sea, the ever-changing, shining winds carry our fragmented dreams to the badlands, Spirit Man. All we are and all we do ends up as lifeless and empty as that forsaken place. The best that you and your little band can hope is that when you die, you move on to eternal rest. Trying to fix what cannot be repaired is futile. Hope only for a swift and permanent end—an end which won't leave you in my sorry state."

Michael lowered his pistol. "Ghost of the Forsaken Ones. I hear you and I understand. Your life was a hard one, full of battle and violence. But that does not need to define your death, does it? Think of it: in every world, yours and mine, death rules over life and conquers it at every turn. You yourself admit this, do you not?"

The ghost hesitated, clearly wary about where Michael was going with this.

"I do," it said at last.

"So then why," Michael said, "do you let the struggles you faced in life continue to define you in death? There is no greater transformation than from life to death, but something in you is stopping that from taking place. Something in you is holding on to all the pain and violence of your life despite how you claim to hate it."

"No," the ghost said, suddenly furious. "You lie, Spirit Man! Why would I condemn myself to this living hell? Why would I strand myself in this half-life, tormented for centuries by all the ills I have done."

Michael put his pistol back into his belt. This ghost, he realized, was no threat to anyone but himself. He was just another sad, lost soul drifting on the chaotic winds of Shook.

"Perhaps," Michael said, "it is because you wish to punish yourself. When you speak, you sound so very, very guilty. You know that you have done wrong, and you trap yourself here as penance."

"No, no, it isn't true," the ghost said, but his voice was feebler now.

Michael took a step forward and rested his hand on the barrel of the ghost's rifle. Slowly, gently, he pushed it down and looked straight into the ghost's eyes.

"I forgive you," Michael said. The ghost's eyes widened. Before it could speak, another voice piped up from behind Michael.

"I forgive you," Trip said.

"We forgive you," said the kids.

     VISION OF THE SPIRIT MAN

"Now," Michael said. "All that's left is for you to forgive yourself."

"Myself..." the ghost said. He seemed at a loss for words, utterly shocked by what had just taken place. The ghostly rifle slipped from his hands and vaporized into mist as it hit the ground. He raised his hands in front of him and stared at them. "So much blood," he said.

Michael nodded. "But you have suffered enough."

The ghost looked at him, then closed his eyes and inhaled. Little by little, starting at the fingertips and the toes, he, too, began to turn into mist. His legs and arms went, then his chest, and finally his head. As the last remnants of him evaporated and blew away on the night wind, Michael heard a whispering sound from the breeze that sounded almost like "thank you."

After that, nothing stirred. Even the wind had stopped. Michael took a deep breath, turned around, and quietly said, "Well. That was...interesting, I guess." A nervous laugh bubbled up out of his throat.

"Wow. That's one way to put it," Trip said. She looked up at him with something like wonder or disbelief in her blue eyes. "How did you know to say all that?"

He shrugged. "I met a strange, luminescent friend out in the desert who gave me some very good life advice. And the ghost was right. We're not so different, really."

Trip touched his arm. "You are. You fight for the right reasons."

"I hope so."

Noel tugged on Trip's arm, barely containing his shivers. "I'm gonna have bad dreams about this—I know I am!"

She mussed his hair and said, "Maybe, but that's why we're all here: to send those nightmares packing. Now let's go get our things; we should start moving before the sun comes up again."

The four of them made their way back into the cave. Michael shot one last look over his shoulder just in case, but there was nothing there. Just a vast expanse of dust and the sound of his own breathing.

Chapter 12

They climbed back into the tank in the pre-dawn chill, just as a detectable but not visible hint of gray first wove its way into the fabric of the sky. The tank's interior, though it smelled a little of sweat, was nice and cool—a refreshing contrast to the last time they had all sat in it. Trip flipped a switch and the diesel engine growled to life. The metal groaned, the treads started turning, and they were off once again, rolling down an old, broken road in the middle of nowhere. Michael hoped he wouldn't have to use the tank's cannon again during this voyage, but knew even as he had the thought exactly how far-fetched it was.

Sure enough, not long after sunrise, Trip spotted something in the distant sky. Michael stooped next to her and peered through the narrow viewport.

"What are those?" he said. "Birds?" About a dozen black specks were approaching across the cloudless blue, but a dozen quickly became two dozen, then three.

"In a manner of speaking," Trip said. "We rather affectionately call them death birds."

"I'm sure I can guess why."

Trip nodded. "Looks like we'll need you back on that gun today."

"Just when I was beginning to really enjoy the day," Michael said, shaking his head and sitting in the gunner's seat. Through the digital viewscreens on his side, he zoomed in on the approaching bogies. They looked like huge ravens with bright yellow claws and beaks big enough to chop a man in half—and he didn't intend to be that man. But, strangely, every last one of them also carried a black satchel in its talons.

"Hey, Trip," Michael said. "What are they carrying?"

"Usually bombs," Trip said. "Let's hope it's bombs."

"There's something worse than bombs?"

"Oh, Michael. You're so naïve. That's what I like about you." With
that, she gunned the engine and veered sharply to the left. "Let's
not make ourselves an easy target now."

Michael tried to open fire on the birds once they were within
range, but they seemed to anticipate each shell before he fired it,
and swooped out of the way just as he pulled the trigger each time.

"I can't hit them!" he shouted.

"Use my rifle!" Trip said.

Michael scooped up the assault rifle and a few extra magazines
and climbed to the hatch. He flung it open and poked his head out,
half expecting to be vaporized on the spot. Luckily, the birds were
still a little ways off, giving him time to line up a few shots. Keeping
his feet on the ladder below, he leaned his elbows against the top
of the tank for stability and took aim. Michael had never fired an
assault rifle before, but he was pretty sure Spirit Man had, so he
relaxed and let muscle memory take over. He looked down the iron
sights, lined up one of the birds, and let out a slow breath. Then he
squeezed the trigger. The burst cut through the morning air and
cut, too, through the death bird. It tried to stay airborne but to no
avail, and spiraled down, down, down until it crashed into the earth.
On impact, the satchel it carried exploded in a great plume of flame,
sending a shockwave of dust careening in every direction. Michael
didn't want to imagine what one of those bombs might do if it landed
on him, so he picked another target and kept firing.

He blasted bird after bird out of the sky, but there were too many
of them and the flock drew ever nearer. He started aiming not for
the birds but for their satchels, hoping to take out more than one
with each shot as they exploded in the air. But the birds, cleverer
than they looked, soon wised up to this strategy and spread out just
far enough that they were only lightly singed by the fiery demise of
their adjacent comrades.

Michael ran out of bullets, reloaded, and kept firing, hoping
he could take out the birds before any of them reached the tank.
Judging by the size of the explosions which rocked the desert

with every bird that fell, even the foot-thick armor on this vehicle wouldn't be enough to survive one of those bombs. He might have succeeded, too, had his rifle not jammed at the last second. All death birds but one had been shot down and blown to smithereens. Michael leveled the rifle at the last target, smiled a little, and pulled the trigger. Click. Nothing. He pulled again. Another click, no bullet. He pulled out the magazine and checked to make sure it wasn't empty, but there were still at least a dozen bullets inside.

"Not great," he said, watching the last bird close the distance with startling speed. He rapped the rifle on the tank to no avail. The jam was really stuck in there, well beyond his ability to clear it without some sort of tool—and what tool that might be, Michael had no idea. He moved to draw his pistol but realized before he did so that he was already too late. At this distance, even if he shot down the bird, it would land close enough to hit the tank.

"Brace yourselves, everyone!" he shouted to the crew below him. Then, as the death bird swooped in for the kill, he dropped back into the tank and slammed the hatch shut behind him. And not a moment too soon.

The blast was tremendous and deafening. It rocked the tank to its very core and Michael felt like the whole thing might just shake apart. He tumbled to the ground and hit his head. The metal around him shuddered and groaned. Sparks flew from the electrical equipment as all the screens inside went dead, plunging all of them into total darkness. After a moment of quiet, Michael patted himself down to make sure he wasn't seriously hurt. The back of his head ached, but otherwise he seemed unharmed.

"Everyone okay?" he said. His voice sounded muffled in his own ears, as if he were underwater.

"I think so," came Trip's voice. "Noel? Nevaeh?"

Michael heard shuffling sounds as the two kids scrambled to their feet.

"That was fun!" they said in unison.

"Well, cherish that memory," Michael said, "because we're not doing it again." He tried to blink away the darkness to no effect.

"Well, I guess I should check out the damage, huh?"

"I'd say so," Trip said.

Michael felt his way to the ladder, climbed to the hatch, and tried to push it open. It didn't move at first, so he gave it a hard push and finally it decided to budge. Daylight flooded the tank as the hatch swung open, blinding as ever. Michael clambered on top of the vehicle and squinted at what had once been their perfectly functional mode of transport. The armor was severely dented and scorched where the bomb had landed, caving in the back left corner of the tank. The tread had been torn to pieces and the half-obliterated wheels sank uselessly into the sand. Michael sniffed and was certain he smelled something burning. He climbed back down.

"Good news and bad news," he said. "Which do we want first?"

"Good news," Nevaeh said.

"Well, that was the last of the death birds, so it looks like we're in the clear."

"And I'll bet we can guess the bad news," Trip said.

Michael nodded. "Looks like we're finishing this journey on foot. This hunk of metal isn't going anywhere."

The four of them clambered out, the kids pointing excitedly at the damage the bomb had inflicted. Michael didn't see what there was to be excited about. The road still stretched on endlessly into the desert, and he wasn't relishing the idea of another long, arduous trek on foot. He glanced at Trip, who seemed to share his apprehension, but what choice did they have? They started walking.

Pretty soon, a wind kicked up and began blowing dust all around them. What was at first a nuisance started to feel more like a genuine danger as the winds picked up more and more speed, accelerating further every second. Before they knew it, the little band of travelers were embroiled in an enormous dust storm which seemed centralized entirely on their location, as if the biggest dust devil in the world were circling their party. Red sand stung Michael's face and hands. Sagebrush and chaparral flattened against the earth all around them. The wind's howling grew in volume until they could barely hear each other's shouts.

"We've got to head back!" Trip shouted. "We can wait this out in the tank!"

Michael was about to agree when another voice arose, carried as if by the wind but firm and powerful and cruel.

"You will never make it in time. Already, my armies descend upon you. Tell me, will your tiny weapons do you any good against hundreds of hungry demons?"

"Who are you?" Michael shouted.

"Foolish Spirit of Man, so forgetful. I am Lord Striker, ruler of the dream world, commander of a thousand dark armies. To me, you and your people are but pests whose hive I have already poisoned. It is long past time I stepped on you."

Trip pulled her rifle off her back and pointed it through the storm, trying to see whatever was approaching.

"Ruler of Shook?" she spat. "In your dreams, buddy."

"Uh, Trip?" Michael said. "Would now be a bad time to mention that that thing is jammed?"

"Why yes, Michael. Yes, it would."

Lord Striker laughed and the land seemed to tremble with his laughter. Only after he had stopped—and the trembling did not—did Michael realize where it was truly coming from. Through the churning dust, a line of dark shapes had appeared and were charging toward him and Trip and the kids. Hundreds of them, at least. Indistinct figures barreling through the storm as if it were nothing to them but a gentle breeze. He raised his pistol and opened fire, but felt the futility of the action as he did so. There were so many of them. He doubted his group had enough bullets to take out even a quarter of their number.

"So long, Spirit of Man," Lord Striker said. "When we meet again, it will be for the last time."

As the figures drew closer, Michael began to discern their horrifying features. They had humanoid bodies, though twisted and hunched and covered in dark fur, rippling with sinewy muscles. But their heads were like those of a bat, with black snouts and sharp teeth. The front line of the advancing force were all foaming at the mouth. Their eyes burned like hot coals and they snarled at the Spirit Man with mouths full of vampire-like fangs. As they marched toward the band of Visionaries, their heavy black boots pounded the earth.

Overhead, ominous dark clouds formed and thickened, and it began to rain heavily down upon the dry, thirsty land. Lightning streaked across the dark purple skies as the dust storm made way for a rainstorm. Fear swept over Michael. The army of bat demons would be upon them in a flash, and the situation seemed desperate. He kept firing, but none of the demons seemed to care when one of their comrades fell to the muddy ground.

"Trip?" he said. "Any ideas?"

Trip had taken out her pistol and was also firing. She turned to him and he saw fear in her eyes as well. "I don't know," she said. "I really have no idea. I don't think we can outrun them." Rain poured down her face, plastering strands of hair against her. She looked like she knew what was about to happen, but didn't want to be the one to say it. She turned to the kids.

"Kids? Come here, stay with me. We're going to be all right."

Michael wished he could believe her, but the charging demons were so close now. They brandished all manner of weapons, from swords to spears to jagged knives and barbed halberds. Some carried improvised weapons like railroad spikes, scythes, and sledgehammers.

When the horde was less than a hundred yards away and still hundreds strong, something happened. A burst of gunfire and ex-plosions ripped through the rain, felling a few dozen of the beasts. Some of them turned around just in time to be run over by a big green monster truck, crushed under its enormous wheels. The truck swerved through the crowd while the mysterious driver unleashed hellfire from the cabin, firing automatic burst after automatic burst, punctuated by the occasional grenade. The demons seemed confused about what to do, uncertain of whether they should continue charging Michael or address this new threat. Michael stared, amazed by the bizarre incongruity between the demon army and the green monster truck. It seemed impossible that both could exist in the same world, let alone the same place, yet here they were, doing battle with one another.

Having finally broken through the front of the bat demon lines, the truck swerved to a stop directly in front of Michael and Trip, splashing them both with brown water. The driver leaned out of the cabin and waved.

"Hey guys," he said. "Nice day, isn't it?"

Michael could barely believe his eyes. "Wally?" he said. Wally was Michael's distant cousin—a once trusted friend that Michael had lost track of over the years and through the course of his travels from one world to another. The last time Michael had seen Wally was on a movie set in California, at the Malibu Creek State Park. If he remembered correctly, they hadn't spoken since they were teenagers. What the hell was Wally doing here? Was it possible that whatever allowed Michael to travel between worlds somehow ran in the family?

Wally leaned over to the passenger side to fire a few bursts and chuck a couple grenades at the still-approaching demon army. Though he'd cut a wide swath through their ranks, hundreds still remained—perhaps as many as a thousand—and the odds still weren't exactly what Michael would call great.

"Long time no see, cousin," Wally said. "Now, I'd love to stay and chat, but I think it's best for all of us if you just hop on in here and we get a move on."

Michael wasn't about to wait around for a second invitation. He scooped up Noel and Trip scooped up Nevaeh, and the four of them climbed up to the truck's cab and slid onto the seat alongside Wally.

"Can you manage one of these?" Wally said, handing an M60 to Trip.

"Absolutely." She leaned out the window, braced the huge machine gun against her shoulder, and started firing as Wally hit the gas. The truck roared to life and took off, leaving the charging demons in its wake. Michael could feel the power of the engine shivering through the cabin, and couldn't help but smile. Saved from the jaws of death once again. He was starting to make a habit out of this.

"How did you know where to find us?" he said.

Wally laughed. "Shook always puts people right where they need to be, didn't you know? If you think about it, this world actually makes a hell of a lot more sense than our world back home."

Michael peered into the rearview mirror at the army of frothing bat demons thirsty for blood.

"Uh, if you say so," he said.

"So Mikey," Wally said. "You seem to have really pissed off Lord Striker."

"It certainly seems that way."

"Still haven't learned how to stay out of trouble, I see."

Michael laughed. "No, I guess not." Despite the rain pouring onto the windshield and the army still in hot pursuit, Michael felt good. For once in his travels he was well and truly not alone. He had companions he trusted, people who could look out for him and for whom he would do the same. He glanced at Trip, drenched from head to toe and still firing the comically large gun behind them. Then at the kids, looking eagerly around the cabin at all the switches and dials and the Point Break bobbleheads on the dashboard. Then at Wally, grinning as wide as ever, his hands resting easily on the huge steering wheel as if he weren't fleeing from a ravenous army, but just out for a leisurely Sunday morning drive.

Michael's good fortune, however, didn't last. Just as it seemed they might be on the verge of losing the bat demons completely, the sky lit up. A lightning bolt slammed down directly onto the truck and everything went dead. The powerful engine sputtered and went silent.

"No, no no no," Wally said. He punched the dashboard, turned the ignition off, then on, then off again. Nothing worked. "Come on, you piece of junk," he said. He flipped a few switches. Nothing. He banged on the steering wheel and cursed, then quickly apologized to the kids for cursing.

"Uh, Wally?" Trip said. "I don't mean to rush you or anything, but they're gaining on us pretty fast. How the hell can they run that fast?"

Wally put his head down on the steering wheel. "It's no use," he said. "Striker just fried the whole setup. Either we run on foot or we just wait for those bastards to climb in and get us."

"I don't like either of those options," Michael said.

Trip opened fire again. In the distance, but rapidly approaching, Michael heard the snarling, slavering horde and felt the tremors of hundreds of boots pounding the earth.

"I hoped it wouldn't come to this," Wally said. He looked at Michael sadly. "They're not coming to kill you, Mikey. They want you alive."

"Me? Why?"

"We don't really have time for this conversation, guys!" Trip said.

"Cousin," Wally said. He pulled a revolver from the glovebox and checked to make sure it was loaded. "Please trust me when I say this is for the best. We can't let you fall into those bastards' claws."

Before Michael could ask what the hell he was talking about, Wally raised the revolver and shot Michael in the head.

Before fading into darkness, Michael had something of an out-of-body experience. He saw the landscape, the rain-drenched desert, the motionless monster truck, the army descending upon it— all as if from a great distance. The bat demons reached the truck and clambered up to the cabin. A battle ensued, but a short one. Before long, the demons regrouped and, having completed their objective, marched away. The rain cleared. A great wind picked up and covered the tracks made by the army, sweeping away any sign that living things had been here at all. As the sun's last rays slipped beneath the dunes, all that remained was an old, empty truck.

Chapter 13

It hurt.

Michael felt like his head was splitting apart and that his heart was doing the same. How could that have happened? How could his own cousin have done that to him? How could Wally have snatched him away from Trip and the kids in an instant? In the place of the deep comradery he had felt only moments ago, there was only a hollow void. He was sure he had seen all of them die, though from a distance, and could not be certain they would come back. But they had to. What was any of this for if they didn't come back? They had to.

As he sat in the vast, empty dark, Michael again understood that he had a choice.

"An easy choice," he said to no one. "How can I give up after coming so far?"

But something nagged at him as he said that. Had he really come so far? So far toward what? He still had no idea who Annihilator was, no idea how to prevent the destruction of the wall and save Shook from becoming like the badlands all over. When he tried to determine what all this struggle had been for, he couldn't put anything into words. But it had meant something, hadn't it? He wasn't just where he started.

Wally's words returned to him. *Shook always puts people right where they need to be.* He knew he needed to trust that, even if it didn't make sense to him. He needed to trust that the invisible path he had been following actually led somewhere and had not simply been taking him in a huge, useless circle.

"Well," he said. "Let's get back to it. Let's see where that path goes."

A sharp pain entered his skull as he said the words, scratching just behind his eyes until everything got fuzzy and started to fade. Just before he lost consciousness again, he realized he was crying. Then everything went away.

Michael lay face down in white sand, which stretched out before him in a wide expanse. The sun was glaring bright, high in the sky, but not nearly so vengeful as the orange desert sun. Rather, its warmth caressed him, coaxing him gently into wakefulness. He groaned, still a little sore, and sat up. A little way off to the left he could see a sparkling blue ribbon of softly rolling surf. The sound of waves against the shore reached him as a tender whisper. Far down the beach, a gleaming white castle towered above bluffs of chalk. White sand dunes stretched forever to the farthest horizon, at once very much like the desert and entirely new. The ocean was a welcome sight after so much time spent in the infinite dryness of the desert.

Michael stood up, feeling a bit unsteady, then took off his shoes and began to walk barefoot along the beach toward the castle. The cool sand was soothing and pleasant against his soles. A low breeze wafted in from the water. The walk would be a long one, but he didn't mind at all.

After an hour or so, or perhaps only a few minutes (it was so difficult to tell, at times), Michael arrived at the base of the castle. It was a simple enough structure, almost like a sand castle made large and constructed of limestone. Two towers soared over the walls and the drawbridge which led to the entrance had been lowered. The whole place seemed practically abandoned, as not a sound emanated from it.

The gates were open, so Michael walked through them into a broad courtyard paved in red tile. Still, he neither saw nor heard a single living soul. There was a huge swimming pool in the middle of the courtyard, in the shape of the figure eight, and a wooden bridge spanned the center portion of the pool, just wide enough for two people to pass one another. Though the pool was large enough for a few hundred swimmers, there were only two lawn chairs in sight.

　　　　　　　　　VISION OF THE SPIRIT MAN

"Who could they possibly be for?" he asked himself. "And why is there no one here?" He walked over to the lawn chairs by the pool side, peered around at the towers to make sure no one was watching him, and eased himself into one of the chairs. He almost expected something to happen as soon as he did, and for a moment he lay tense, waiting for whatever it was to come out and attack him. Then he relaxed, took a deep breath, and stretched his arms and legs out as far as he could. He could see the ocean through the open gates, and watched the waves roll in, one after another, sliding over the sands of the beach and gradually retreating to make way for the next one. Though he had, ostensibly, only just awoken, the sound made Michael acutely aware of how tired he actually was. All those days of marching across the desert washed over him all at once and he realized, even if he tried, he likely would be quite unable to leave that chair.

Soon enough, Michael's eyes became heavy, and he let himself relax into a soft, welcoming sleep. In no time, he began to dream. In his dream, the sky had become very dark and gloomy. Bolts of lightning flashed, and then a massive black cat appeared in the sky, with eyes as yellow as the sun and teeth flashing white as fear against the sparkling black of its fur. Great fangs bared, the huge predator yowled its challenge and bolted out of the sky with fiendish ferocity, racing toward Michael, still prone on the lawn chair.

Michael tried to scream but couldn't. He struggled to move or defend himself but he was paralyzed. The cat loped through the sky above Michael's head and lunged at him, jaws agape. Just before it devoured him, he snapped back into wakefulness. He was breathing heavily and sweating a little. He sat up and looked around, finally daring to look at the sky to see if his dream had become reality. But there was only blue sky, a few clouds, and no black cat.

"You were just dreaming, that's all," came a voice.

Surprised, Michael's gaze snapped to the source of the sound—the lawn chair directly across from him where he could have sworn, a moment ago, no one had been sitting. Lounging there now was a strange young woman with a very amused expression on her face.

She wore an expensive-looking satin gown and had an amethyst-colored flower tucked into the hair over one ear.

"Who are you?" Michael said.

"You can call me Magellan. This is my father's castle, so you can imagine my surprise at having a visitor."

"I'm sorry to barge in, I didn't think anyone lived here."

She shook her head and laughed. "No imposition at all. I can't even remember the last time we had visitors, and it gets awfully lonely out here by the sea. Too much time to oneself to think and dwell on everything they're missing out on by being here and not somewhere else."

"Well, here seems like a pretty nice place to be," Michael said. "Especially compared to a few of the other places I've visited."

"Oh, it's very nice at first," Magellan said. "But after years and years, it becomes terribly boring."

"I suppose I can understand that. Oh, I'm so sorry, I forgot to even introduce myself."

Magellan laughed again and waved him off. "Don't be silly, of course I know who you are, Spirit Man. I'd be a pretty poor resident of Shook if I didn't know that."

"Geez, does everyone know who I am?"

"More or less. You're something of a celebrity here, you know."

"Well, all I've gotten for my celebrity status so far is a whole lot of enemies, and even more trouble," Michael said.

"Don't worry, you'll find neither here."

"I can't tell you what a relief that is," he said, then looked around once more, as if someone else might have appeared while he wasn't looking. "Is there any chance someone else passed through here before me? A woman and a couple of children, about ten and eleven years old?"

Magellan thought for a moment, then shook her head. "I don't believe so. Like I said, you're the first person I've seen who isn't my father in quite some time. I have to say it's a nice change of pace." She jumped suddenly to her feet. "That reminds me, you should meet my father. I'm sure he'll be just as thrilled as I am to make your acquaintance."

"Right, right, of course," Michael said. "Lead away."

They walked together to the castle, then up a flight of stairs made of white marble with streaks of gold in it. At the top of the stairs were two huge glass doors from the Plaza Hotel in New York City, inlaid with beautiful gold swirls and designs. Magellan opened the doors and they walked into the main hall of the castle. After a few steps, Michael stopped in the middle of the great hall, and looked around in awe and wonder. There were huge white Roman columns on both sides of the hall that rose up to a dome of stained-glass angels, shimmering in the daylight.

"This is incredible," Michael said.

"Yes, it is. Wait here," she said. "I'll let my father know you've arrived." She turned and walked away down a long hall. "Don't worry, I'll be right back!"

Michael studied the gorgeous architecture and stained glass work, patiently waiting for Magellan to return. He soon realized that the images depicted on the glass were a recreation of Pieter Bruegel's *The Fall of the Rebel Angels* painting. Saint Michael and his fellow angels cast down Lucifer and his rebellious comrades, expelling them forever from the heavens. Something about it struck Michael as oddly significant, beyond the obvious beauty of the work. Why this painting in this particular space, at this particular time? Trying to piece it all together felt too big a task, so he let it go.

Soon, Magellan breezed back into the great hall. "My father is very eager to meet you," she said. "Come, he's waiting in his study."

Michael followed her across the huge hall of the castle and down a long, winding hallway. They came to a beautifully carved door which bore an engraved brass plate reading LIBRARY.

Magellan opened the oak door and they walked into the room together. It was large and fitted with floor-to-ceiling bookshelves housing thousands of volumes. The only wall which wasn't laden with books was made entirely of huge windows overlooking the ocean below. As though these were made of faceted crystal, the afternoon sun which shone through the windows created tiny rainbows on the library's many surfaces—red, pink, and purple streaked the floor and patches of yellow, orange, green, and blue decorated the books that lined the opposing wall. A richly colored Persian rug was spread between two blood-red armchairs, which stood in front of a massive fireplace with an intricately carved mantle. Above the fireplace and on either side of it, huge abstract paintings featured swirling colors and inquisitive, disembodied eyes. Taken together, the furnishings, artwork, and radiant sunlight impressed Michael almost as much as the great hall itself.

Magellan stepped over to where her father sat behind a wide, polished mahogany desk. She kissed his cheek by way of greeting. Michael was surprised to recognize that the desk and the part of the room where the old man sat looked exactly like his own office at Seymour Mansion. Once again, he had the strange sense that he could almost remember something very important...something which remained just outside his mental grasp, no matter how hard he tried to focus on it. Then Magellan waved him over, and he snapped out of his trance and made his way over to the desk.

"This is my father Jacques," she said.

Jacques was a very tall man. When he stood to greet Michael, he rose almost a whole head above him—noteworthy given that Michael was quite a tall person himself. Jacques was a classically distinguished-looking gentleman, well-dressed in a tailored suit, tanned and radiantly healthy. Though he must have been in his fifties at least, he didn't look a day over forty. He moved with the grace of an athlete, and his handshake was firm and warm with generous energy. He ran his fingers through his long, silver-gray hair as he invited them to sit down with him.

"Magellan tells me that you are the Spirit Man," Jacques said. "If that is true, then I've been waiting for this moment all my life."

"I am," Michael said. He watched the man's features as he spoke. Something was slightly amiss but he couldn't place what it was at first. The man seemed to not quite be looking at him, even when he was. Only gradually did Michael come to understand that he was blind.

   VISION OF THE SPIRIT MAN

Jacques smiled, seemingly aware of Michael's realization, but he said nothing of it. "Hungry, Spirit Man?" he asked.

"Starving," Michael said.

"I'll take care of it," Magellan said, bouncing to her feet. She sashayed through an ornately carved door, and in what seemed like only seconds, came skipping back with a big silver tray laden with finger sandwiches, assorted desserts, and drinks. She put the tray down on a table in a small sitting area of the library and gave a little mock curtsey.

"All right," Jacques said. "Shall we?"

The three of them sat around the tray. Jacques's hands fluttered quickly over the tray, locating points along its edge, and observing the different shapes of the little plates. He picked up a slice of delicious looking Southern-style pecan pie and dug into it with a silver dessert fork.

Michael paused only long enough to decide whether to begin with the thick and inviting stuffed little sandwiches or go directly to the confections. He picked up a sandwich in each hand and devoured each in four big bites, relishing their delicate flavor. He couldn't say for certain what was in each of them, but knew without a doubt that he could eat an entire platter of them. Then he picked up a tall, frosty silver tumbler of orange juice and sipped it, finding it to be the freshest he had ever tasted.

"Where did all this come from?" he said.

"I just made it," Magellan said.

"But...you were only gone for a moment, weren't you?"

Jacques patted Michael's arm. "Haven't you learned by now that there's no sense questioning such things, Spirit Man? Just enjoy and eat up. You'll need all of your strength for tomorrow's long journey." He took a bite out of his pie.

"Journey?" Michael said, trying a fat chocolate brownie smeared with marzipan.

"Try the little crab salad sandwiches," Mr. Champs encouraged. "I really shouldn't indulge in such rich food, but what the hell—I've made it this far, haven't I?" He grinned and popped a little creampuff into his mouth. "You should definitely try one of those too."

Michael did. It was the lightest and fluffiest pastry he had ever tasted, and when he bit into it, it gushed the most perfectly spiced cream filling.

"But what journey, sir?" he said. He was already dreading the prospect of having to leave this place—and this food—behind so soon.

"Are we ready for the coffee?" Jacques asked. No sooner had he said this than Magellan appeared at Michael's shoulder with three steaming mugs. "Ah, thank you sweetheart," Jacques said, taking a sip. He set the mug carefully in front of him and turned to Michael.

"Magellan will take you to the wall tomorrow morning," he said. "Isn't that why you have come all this way?"

"The wall..." Michael said. A knot formed in his gut. "Why do I need to go to the wall? Shouldn't I be looking for Annihilator to make sure the Saviors can't tear it down?" He looked up at Magellan, who turned away from him.

Jacques sipped at his coffee quietly for a time, a frown darkening his features. Then he set his mug down again and took a deep breath.

"I am afraid they have already found their key," he said. "Even as we speak, they are bringing the Annihilator to the wall and preparing it to speak its true name and send the wall crashing down. If that happens, oases like this will cease to exist. All of Shook will become a blasted wasteland, uninhabitable except by the most rugged and ruthless of sorts."

Michael winced. Had he failed, then? If the Saviors had already located the Annihilator....He shook off the thought and the creeping pessimism it brought. If Jacques said there was still time, there was still time. He had to believe that.

"You think we can still stop them?" Michael said.

Jacques nodded. "Only if we act quickly. But prepare yourself. The wall is manned by thousands of slaves who work night and day—unto their very deaths—at the behest of the Saviors and their leader. Piece by piece, they chip away at it, as they have been forced to do for years. When you arrive, you will see so much human suffering,

   VISION OF THE SPIRIT MAN

sorrow, and pain that you will wish that you could close your eyes and be blind forever, like me. That is the wall."

There was a long moment of silence in the room, and then Magellan said, "My father is getting tired now. We should let him get some rest—you two can talk more later." She walked to her father and gently kissed his forehead.

Jacques stood and shook Michael's hand once more. "It is good to finally meet you, Spirit Man. I only hope you are able to do what I believe you are capable of doing."

"Likewise," said Michael.

Then Magellan led Michael from her father's room, and they walked together through the great hall. "Come on, I'll show you to your room," she said.

They strolled in companionable silence until they came to a carved oak door which opened onto a small but elegantly furnished room. The narrow bed was draped in crisp white linens and flanked by mahogany night tables. A thick red Persian rug covered the stone floor, and the late afternoon sunlight shone brightly through a small, leaded glass window.

"I hope you like it," Magellan said. Then she kissed him lightly on both cheeks. "See you in the morning."

Michael smiled as she went down the long hallway and disappeared around a corner. Then he closed the door and watched as the red and gold light of sunset flooded the room through the crystal panes of the window. After his afternoon nap, he wasn't feeling particularly tired, but the bed was simply too inviting to resist. He lay down on it and found that it was every bit as comfortable as it appeared—and then some. It wouldn't hurt to rest a while longer, would it? After all, he'd need his strength for the journey tomorrow. Before he could even finish the thought, he was fast asleep.

When he awoke, candles were burning in the dark room, their reflections winking in the window panes like the eyes of watchers in the dark beyond. The bedroom door stood ajar, and a cool breeze wafted through the room. Michael peered down toward his feet. A black cat was curled up on his legs and was purring loudly. It was the same black cat he had seen in his terrible dream, only much smaller—the size of a domestic feline, rather than a great sky predator. It stirred and for a moment Michael feared it would leap at him again. But it just stretched, then jumped down from the bed and slipped from the room with characteristic feline stealth.

Wide awake now, something compelled Michael to toss aside his covers and follow the cat down the hallway, around the corner to a spiral staircase, and then up the winding column, round and round as fast as he could climb. Twenty, forty, sixty, one hundred, two hundred, three hundred steps, and the staircase wound on. Following the cat, Michael climbed and climbed. Though he had very long legs, and took very long strides, the cat somehow always managed to stay ahead of him. When he finally reached the top of the spiral staircase, he realized where he was: at the very top of one of the castle's towers.

The chamber at the top of the tower was lit only by the thin glow of the moon, which filtered in through a series of small windows to cast eerie shadows in the corners. The black cat stood only a few feet away, near the dark form of a low archway, its bright yellow eyes piercing the darkness. It turned and stepped into the gloom, leaving just the tip of its tail visible. Michael followed it, crouching so he wouldn't hit his head on the rough stones of the arch.

The darkness in the tiny room was thick, but the moonlight cast enough of a glow for Michael to see. There were windows all the way around, and Michael had a perfect view of the night sky. He had never seen so many stars before, so perfectly undiluted by any form of light pollution. The depth of the sky was dizzying, and he could only look for so long before feeling like he was falling into that vast cold blackness. He turned back to the contents of the room. There, in the center, stood an altar of white marble on which rested a large, thick book. He couldn't make out the title in the dim moonlight, but a stub of candle and a matchbook sat beside it. He lit the candle, and saw that the cover on the book read: *The Crack in the Wall* by Jacques Cornwall Champs.

Michael carefully opened the book and was surprised to find that it was written in Braille. Every page of the immense volume was covered with rows of raised dots. Of course. The poet was blind. It was only the candle that was out of place.

Michael touched his fingertips to the dots and ran them across the page, surprised to realize he actually understood the words. He did not remember learning Braille, yet here he was, reading it with perfect fluency. He blew out the candle, let the dark take over the room once more, and read the poem through his fingers:

CITY OF DREAMERS

Moonlit footprints in damp

sand are as

temporary

as a city built of

hard, real things. Steel

rusts, wood rots, concrete cracks

and

inhabitants

turn to dust in their

sleep. Such are the fragile realities

of reality. But dreams

are made of much sterner stuff

and a city of dreamers falls to no storm

nor earthquake. A city of dreamers

can build a wall in a day or tear

it down in an instant

if only they know who they are

and who rules their city.

A city of dreamers is a shape-

shifting city, built of clay

and atop clay, waiting

for a shaper's hand, firm and

certain, to give it life.

Michael removed his hand from the pages. Was this the City of Dreams he had been searching for all this time? Just some poem in an old book? If so, he wished it had been a little clearer about what he was supposed to learn from it. Was this meant to help him save the wall in some way? As he wondered this, a sudden single gust of wind swirled through the tiny tower room. It flipped the pages of the thick book and slammed the cover shut. Michael jumped, then scrambled to re-light the candle. For a moment the flickering of the flame made the title seem to dance on the book's cover, and then a capering little gust blew it out, plunging the room into darkness again.

The thin sliver of moon had vanished from the sky, and the icy pinpricks of the stars offered no relief from the fearsome sudden blindness of the night. In the darkness, Michael sensed that he was not alone. He listened for the purring of the cat, but heard only silence. He held his breath and listened again, and then he thought he heard something or someone breathing in the room.

"Who's there?" he whispered. A chill crept up his spine and he felt his heart beating in his chest. He tried to scoff at his own foolishness, but still found himself fearing that the black cat of his dreams would leap out of the dark shadows and attack him.

Michael turned his head slowly, seeking the source of the presence he felt more than heard. Breathing deeply, he forced his jangled nerves to calm. Yes—yes, there was somebody breathing in the room with him. From the depths of the darkest shadow in the room, an unseen shape lurked. Michael closed his eyes and tried to listen and feel and smell. He wondered if the cat had transformed itself into a larger thing, a beast ready to pounce on him and kill him again and again. He opened his eyes and looked around for a weapon. He wanted to strike out and try to destroy whatever horror awaited him, but all that revealed itself was the book. It was heavy enough, at least. He reached for it and, just as he did, heard a soft footstep on the stone. He grabbed the book and swung it through the air, connecting with nothing. A dark shape jumped out of the way just in time. Before he could swing again, a familiar voice came from the darkness.

"Michael, Michael, it's only me."

     VISION OF THE SPIRIT MAN

"Magellan?" he said. "What are you doing here?"

"I heard you on the stairs," she said. "And I...I thought you were leaving without me."

She embraced him, then quickly released him, as if embarrassed. "Um, I should get some rest. We have a long way to go tomorrow." With that, she turned and disappeared once more into the dark, leaving Michael confused but not at all displeased about the encounter.

"Weird woman," he said to himself, and chuckled. Then he set the book back in its place and walked down the stairs to his room.

Chapter 14

The gentle rolling of the surf roused Michael the next morning with the utmost care and gentleness. A soft breeze sifted through his open window as the sun's first rays peeked into his room. He had to remind himself where he was, having been so many different places over the past days and weeks. When he remembered the castle, Magellan, and the pristine beach all around, he sank deeper into his bed. He didn't want to leave. He didn't want to make another long, dangerous journey to the wall where, if Jacques was to be believed, only horrors awaited him. At last, however, he forced himself to rise and get dressed. There was too much at stake to be lounging about.

He heard footsteps on the stairs, followed by a light tap at his door. Magellan peeked her head into his room.

"Breakfast is ready, Michael. Come join us."

He nodded and followed her downstairs to the great hall, where a huge wooden table had been set with all manner of foods. Jacques was already seated, and gestured at the platters of everything from fluffy scrambled eggs with fried potatoes, to smoked fish in cream, to gooseberry crepes and apricot empanadas and beyond. It was beyond a feast for the three of them, and he couldn't imagine that they would even be able to make a dent in the offerings.

Magellan placed a small bowl of water and a towel at her father's elbow. "Here, Father—no need to fuss with your knife and fork. Just use this washbasin." She smiled at Michael and draped a napkin over her father's lap.

"Don't mind me, Spirit Man," Jacques said. "I just enjoy my food so much more when I eat with fingers—touching it lets me experience it in another way."

Michael watched him pick up a syrup-soaked pancake, smear it with whipped butter, roll it like a burrito and bite off a big mouthful.

"It looks like your method is better all the way around," Michael said, and followed suit. Soon the three of them were eating breakfast companionably, licking their fingers and chatting in the late morning sunlight.

As he ate, Michael wished he had another mouth and two more hands with which to enjoy the meal. He picked up another piece of crispy bacon.

Jacques chuckled. "Someone must really be hungry. Don't they feed you in the world you come from?"

"Not like this," Michael said, grinning. "Back home, people are just so damn busy they don't have time to eat a good breakfast."

"What a shame," Jacques said, with genuine sympathy.

"Father and I eat all our meals together. Don't we, Father?" Magellan said.

"Yes, we do, honey," he said. "I look forward to eating with my daughter every day, Spirit Man, just as much as writing my poems, taking my walks on the beach, and best of all, having Magellan read to me, way, way into the night."

"It sounds like a beautiful life," Michael said. The ache at having to leave this place so soon throbbed again. He desperately hoped that somehow, someday, he would find it again—and perhaps be allowed to stay for much longer next time.

"It is. A peaceful life, too. I wish I could offer you the same, but alas, circumstances intercede." He shook his head mournfully, then went on. "This trek may be the most important of your lives. After this wonderful breakfast, you must begin your journey to the wall." He paused dramatically and Magellan took a sip from her tea. "Magellan knows the way, and she can take you. It will take days to get there, but Magellan knows places that will be safe to stop at night. Don't you, dearest?"

"Of course, Father," she said.

"Go to the wall," Jacques said earnestly, and for a moment Michael was sure the man could see right through him. "Stop the Saviors and their leader. If you fail, God help us, I fear our home will forever vanish from the face of the earth."

"I'll make sure that doesn't happen," Michael said, and he almost believed it.

When they were finished, the sun had barely risen above the horizon. Magellan got up and kissed her father on his cheek. "Goodbye for now. I love you, Father," she said.

Michael rose too, and shook Jacques's hand with deep affection. "Goodbye, sir. I won't let you down." He still wasn't even sure what he was supposed to do once he found Annihilator, but he hoped he could handle whatever came his way.

Jacques nodded. "Be careful," he said.

Magellan had packed canteens of cool water, ham sandwiches, and dried fruit and pastries into a small leather knapsack. She handed it to Michael and he swung it over his shoulder. Then they were off, leaving that wonderful place far behind.

They walked down the endless beach and for hours Michael was able to stop himself from turning around. When he finally looked back, the castle was no more than a white speck in the distance, barely distinguishable from the plain of white sand. The sun rose high into the sky but the breeze off the ocean kept them cool. Magellan walked ahead of Michael, scampering barefoot along the very edge of the surf. The dark, thick waves of hair perfectly matched the twisted spirals of sea-soaked driftwood that littered the shore, as if she were some sort of goddess of the sea.

They reached a break in the beach around sunset, a point which curved out a few hundred feet into the surf. The beach beyond was made of red dunes which quickly became tall rocky bluffs. As he watched, a flock of pelicans swept in from the dunes and began to dive into the surf off the point. In seconds, each bird came to the surface with a huge fish in its beak. He watched in fascination as each one flipped its fish into the air, caught it head first, and gulped it down with a smile and a wink.

Michael turned back toward the beach, but Magellan was nowhere in sight. Alarm flooded his chest. He could see all the way down the white beach, but there was no Magellan. He looked

    VISION OF THE SPIRIT MAN

down the red beach as well and didn't see her there either. Then he spotted patches of olive green and yellow between two of the nearest dunes—little gnarled trees and tall dried reeds. He started toward the closest clump of brush just as Magellan stepped out from behind it and waved to him.

"Magellan, you can't just disappear like that," he said. "I thought you were lost. Anything can happen out here, don't you know that?"

"Silly man," she said with a grin. "We're safe here. There's nothing that can harm us for miles and miles. We'll spend the night among the dunes, and then tomorrow we'll head out again. Come on now, follow me."

She stepped into a clump of the tall reeds, and Michael followed her into a hidden, shadowy world shaded with damp, overgrown jungle. Incredibly, as they made their way through the undergrowth, a great primordial forest sprang up all around them, and Michael marveled at the height of the sycamore and cypress trees. Nothing so tall had been visible from the beach, and yet, as they walked along, the jungle engulfed them and grew taller and thicker with each step. As the reeds and wide wet leaves slipped over his arms and face, it seemed almost inevitable that somewhere among the overgrowth, a big tiger or lion waited to leap out and devour him. Only Magellan's calm certainty kept his unease at bay.

The reeds parted in front of them and Michael looked out over a little clearing—a peaceful jungle oasis ringed in tall plants, with a red dune rising up behind it. Right in the middle stood a little hut of bamboo, with a rough floor of wide boards and a roof made of thatch.

"Do you like it?" she asked, gazing up at him expectantly, waiting for an answer.

"Yes, absolutely. It's so simple and cozy. Is it yours?"

"No, of course not. It's my father's place," she said with a happy little laugh. "Come on, let's get settled in for the night."

Michael squinted at the horizon, where the sun was melting from yellow to a deep red as it slid into the water.

"Do you want me to help with anything?" he said.

"Sure—you can help me air out the bedding."

They went into the little hut and Michael took in the simple amenities. A wide, graceful bed with a carved headboard stood in the middle of the room and took up most of the space. To the left of the bed, a wide buffet and a set of shelves held a washbasin and pitcher, a few rustic plates and cups, a lantern, and a small stock of canned goods. To the right stood a large armoire, a wood burning stove, and a small pile of logs. A narrow table and two chairs were placed near the stove.

Magellan set to work. She went to the trunk at the foot of the bed, took out a large feather duvet, and carried it out into the little clearing. Unfolding it, she gripped two of its corners. Michael took hold of the opposite end and helped her shake it out, flapping the cotton folds mightily in the mild breeze. A swirling cloud of dust rose in the air, and Michael began to sneeze and cough. Then a gust of the sea breeze swept over the trees and into the clearing and the cloud of dust disappeared in seconds, leaving the air freshly tinged with the salty scent of the tide.

"Works every time! Don't even need a broom!" she said.

They took the bedding into the little house, stripped the dust cover off the bed, and laid down fresh sheets from the armoire. Magellan tucked the end of the duvet under the foot of the bed. "Why don't you pull the table and chairs out?" she suggested. "That way, we can eat together while the sun goes down."

Michael did as he was asked and dragged the little table and chairs out into the clearing. Next, he took the sandwiches, fruit, and water from their backpack and laid them out, along with plates and mugs for the water. He found a pair of candlesticks in the armoire, and lit them with a wooden match from the box on the stove. By the time Magellan joined him, he had created quite a picturesque picnic spot in the middle of the jungle.

Magellan came to the door and surveyed his efforts. "This is lovely! Better than the fanciest of restaurants."

Michael poured water in her mug and then offered her a pastry. "These are a little banged up from being carried around in a backpack all day, but they'll still taste good." In a strange way, he felt self-conscious and awkward, in a way that he hadn't felt in a long time. Despite the bizarre, danger-laden circumstances, he felt like he was on a weird sort of date. He wondered if Magellan was thinking the same thing, but if she was, she didn't let on. He picked up a sandwich and did his best to eat it slowly, even though his stomach growled in protest. As they ate, the sun breathed its last warmth across the world, turning the narrow swatch of sky that was visible through the trees a dark purple-red.

Magellan looked at Michael very seriously. "This was the easy part," she said. "Tomorrow, we'll enter the badlands."

"Don't we have to go past the wall to get there?" he said.

She shook her head. "There's a...shortcut, I guess you'd call it. An accidental opening between two places that aren't supposed to be connected. We'll just slip through there and no one will be the wiser. It's our only chance of getting to the wall in time."

Michael nodded. "I trust you."

"Good! I would certainly hope so."

After they finished eating, they sat in the cozy glow of the candlelight for a long while, watching the stars above. Finally, Magellan rose.

"We really should get some sleep," she said.

Michael collected their dishes and they went inside.

"Is there another blanket or something?" he said. "I can sleep on the floor—you take the bed."

"Don't be silly." Magellan took off her shoes and slid into the bed, then patted the spot next to her. "It's plenty big enough for both of us."

Michael shrugged, left his shoes on the floor, and climbed into the other side of the bed. It wasn't quite as comfortable as the one in the castle, but it was close. And besides that, the company was nice.

Within minutes, he heard Magellan's breathing slow to a steady rhythm and knew she had fallen asleep. He was tired from all their walking but lay awake for some time, listening to the sound of her soft breaths.

Michael dreamed a huge black panther walking along the red beach in the middle of the night. It was so dark that the beach was black, the sky was black, and even the sea was black; only the faint glint of muted starlight reflecting off the animal's glossy hide made it visible. The great jungle cat opened its mouth and roared into the night.

When Michael woke up the next morning, Magellan was gone. Still half-asleep, he thought she might be outside setting the table for breakfast. He stretched and got out of bed, then noticed that the remaining fruit and pastries they had packed for their journey were still in the knapsack. He called out, but there was no answer. Pulling on his shoes and trying to tamp down the worry rising inside him, he went outside, hoping there might be a spring or a swimming hole she had gone to. But as he poked around in the nearby jungle and called her name a few more times, he began to feel a sense of dread that he couldn't keep at bay. The beginnings of fear began to bubble somewhere deep in his blood.

He looked up at the sun, and he could tell which direction the sea was, but he was not sure he could find his way back through the thick jungle to the hut if he left it. Instead, he scrambled to the top of the big red sand dune behind the hut. A massive tree thrust itself skyward from the crest of the dune; the perfect lookout spot. Hauling himself from one knotty branch to another, Michael began to climb. In a few minutes, he could see over the gnarled trees and the waving reeds; in the distance, the surf rolled in on the rust-red beach.

"Magellan!" he cried. He looked up and down the beach for her. His voice was lost in the vastness of the surf, and not even a pelican answered his cry. How could he have been so careless? How could he have lost track of her on only the second day of their journey? He scanned the horizon left to right then right to left and back again, over and over, but she was nowhere to be found. Finally, the muscles in his calves and thighs began to throb and tingle, and he was forced to climb down from his perch. Alone once again, he returned to the hut.

Chapter 15

Only when he sat once again at the table outside the hut to think did Michael notice the pawprints. Two sets of giant prints, like those belonging to an oversized cat, led directly to the hut and then away, off toward the beach. The panther. Michael cursed. He should have seen it coming. Of course the dreams had meant something!

He jumped to his feet, gathered up his things, and followed the tracks. There was no way to know how long ago Magellan had been taken, but the longer he delayed, the lower his chances of finding her would be. In a moment, he burst through the vegetation and onto the beach. Here, the tracks were impossible to miss. A single set of prints marching across the otherwise unmarked sand. The prints were perfect where the sand had been moist. Michael followed the trail for a hundred yards or so, at which point the tracks veered sharply toward the sea. They led straight into the surf and disappeared. Michael shook his head and dashed up and down the beach, searching for a place where they might reappear.

"No, no, no," he said.

It was no use. There were no more tracks to follow. All he could do was continue along the beach and hope that somewhere, somehow, the prints would emerge from the ocean and lead him to Magellan. Even the wall seemed unimportant now. All that mattered was finding her and rescuing her from whatever creature had stolen her away.

Michael walked for miles. The sand turned to rocks, and the rocks became the beginning of cliffs. The surf fell farther and farther away as he climbed the steep incline but still no tracks appeared, nor any other sign he could discern. It was as if the panther had simply vanished. His legs ached from the increasingly difficult hike, but he refused to give up. If there was any chance at all he could help, he would walk until he dropped dead of exhaustion.

As it turned out, the Saviors got him first.

The Saviors came in a pack, howling and screeching obscenities. Some drove their caravan of junk jeeps and dune buggies, or clung to the sides of the vehicles, while others ran alongside in a galloping leathery horde. Michael heard them approaching from a ways off but he was so exhausted by that time that he knew he wouldn't be able to mount much of a defense. He tried to reach into himself to call upon the Shadow Runner or the Blade Master but by the time he even began the process, the Saviors were all around him, tires skidding on the wet rocks of the bluffs as they slalomed to a stop. The biggest man, who appeared to be in command of the group, was in the jeep closest to Michael. Like the others, he was dressed in old, patched army camouflage fatigues, but his were less ragged than theirs, and he wore bright bands of gold braids around his sleeves like a naval officer.

He glared at Michael from behind his white mask, casually stepped out of his jeep, and leveled a sawed-off shotgun at Michael's chest.

"Spirit Man," he said. "Pleasure to make your acquaintance."

"Likewise," Michael said. He looked around for some sort of escape, but there were just too many Saviors with too many guns pointed at him. He knew if he made even a single move, he'd be chopped into a thousand pieces in an instant.

"The Madame would very much like to have a word with you," the Savior said.

"Who the hell is The Madame?" Michael said.

The Saviors began to laugh and hoot but their leader quickly silenced them with a gesture.

"The Madame rules the badlands," he said. "And pretty soon, that means she'll rule all of Shook. So you'd best not keep her waiting if you know what's good for you." Then he signaled to the nearest of his Savior troops. "All right, squad, round him up and let's get him back to the camp. Now!"

With a whoop, six of the soldiers leaped forward and pounced on Michael before he even had time to twitch. They flipped him over,

    VISION OF THE SPIRIT MAN

bound his hands and feet like a calf at a rodeo, then snatched him up and carried him like a trophy over their heads, passing him from one set of hands to another until they dumped him into an old army truck.

The leader looked down at Michael and said, "Don't get too comfy. We're only going to keep you alive long enough for The Madame to kill you herself. She's got a special something that's supposed to kill Visionaries permanently, and the boys and I are all pretty excited about it. If what I'm told is true, this will hardly be the first time she's used it."

Then the leader laughed and walked away. One by one the vehicles started up, belching diesel fumes into the air, and got moving. Michael looked up to see that he wasn't alone in the back of this truck. The benches on either side of the bed were lined with Saviors, all of them watching him, weeping over their masks, and pointing rifles at his head.

The leader yelled something from his jeep and the truck lurched into motion. The wide-set tractor tires grabbed the slick rocks and the truck crawled up the side of the incline like a huge desert beetle. It bumped over every loose rock, bouncing Michael around and bruising him over and over again. He desperately hoped this wasn't going to be a long ride.

"Where are we going?" he asked.

The Saviors just stared at him for a while before one finally deigned to answer the question.

"The wall," was all he said.

Well, that was one way to get there, Michael figured. He tossed out his half-formed escape plans, all of which would have almost certainly ended with him full of bullet holes. Maybe, just maybe, these same Saviors had captured Magellan and taken her to the wall as well. Or maybe she had escaped the mysterious panther and was even now searching for him. Either way, the wall was the smartest place to be. Staying alive once he got there would be another sticky issue, but he decided to worry about that once he arrived.

Michael looked from one silent mask to the next, probing for some hint of weakness. He found none. Every pair of eyes was as stony as the last, despite the tears perpetually leaking from them. He got the clear sense that this wouldn't be the sort of situation he could talk his way out of. Evidently, one of the Saviors got tired of Michael watching them all the time, because he stood up, spit on Michael, then kicked him hard in the head with a steel-toed boot. Everything went black.

Consciousness returned slowly and painfully. Michael groaned and opened his eyes to a dark, blurry landscape. He realized he was once more in the badlands. Black stone stretched in every direction with not a single sign of life. Dead, petrified trees reached for the churning gray sky.

One of the Saviors chuckled. "I hope you're ready to see something amazing, Spirit Man." He and one of his compatriots wrenched Michael to his feet and pointed him in the direction the truck was traveling. "A thing of beauty, isn't it?"

Up ahead, still several miles off, was the wall. It was as vast and imposing as the first time he saw it, but there was something more this time. He squinted as what looked like cobwebs stretching all the way up to the top of the wall. Using the vision the orb had given him, he was able to get a clearer picture. Not cobwebs at all. Scaffolding. It stretched from the base of the wall to the top, and at every level were dozens of men and women with iron collars around their necks and pickaxes in their hands, chipping away.

Everywhere he looked, Michael saw the tangled structures of scaffolding, ramps, pulleys, and cranes; everywhere, masses of people dressed in rags worked under the supervision of whip-wielding Saviors. He saw one worker collapse from exhaustion, and when a few whippings didn't rouse him, the Savior overseer simply picked him up, detached his collar from the chain, and hurled him off the scaffolding. Michael, horrified, followed the man's descent all the way to the ground. There, at the base of this wall, was a sprawling slum, row after row of tents and shacks, all surrounded

     VISION OF THE SPIRIT MAN

by enormous barbed-wire fences.

"The camp at the bottom," Michael said. "What is that?"

"That's the Charnel House," the Savior said. "We'll introduce you soon enough."

The caravan rumbled on, bumping over the barely-maintained road as it approached the camp. Soon enough, they passed through the first round of fences and entered the outskirts of the Charnel House. Emaciated workers peered out from their ramshackle huts, eyes wide with fear and sharp with hunger. Gradually, the density of the hovels grew until they were packed so tightly together than Michael imagined the occupants barely had room to lay down in their own homes. Amid all these cramped residences were drainage ditches leading to sludge pools and huge, rust-streaked factories which sent a pall of greasy brown smoke into the sky.

As they drove through the densely populated garbage dump, Michael noticed that no kids played between the tumbled-down huts. Instead, there were long lines of small children, naked or wearing only a rag diaper, carrying long poles crossed into X's, with one end on the shoulder of a child in front and one end held by a child in the rear. A bucket hung from the middle of each cross. The endless lines moved along like a trail of ants, carrying buckets of water one way and buckets of refuse the other.

"Do these kids even know their parents?" Michael asked.

The Saviors all laughed. The one holding Michael leaned in close. He could smell the sour stink of his breath.

"We're much more practical than that," the Savior said. "The whelps are taken to nurseries at birth, where they are raised and trained to work. Good little grubbers get water duty, like those you see."

"And the bad ones?"

"Tunnel rats—hauling rocks and scum out of small, dark, wet places that have a tendency to collapse on you. Many die, but not more than we're willing to lose."

As they approached the base of the wall itself, the height of it seemed impossible. It was higher than some mountain ranges, and though not perfectly vertical, it was incredibly steep and criss-crossed with narrow ledges and ramps leading ever upward. The truck lurched to a stop, and the white-faced Savior soldiers rose from their benches, leaped to the ground, and began to line up side by side. The last two out of the truck carried Michael with them and threw him onto the ground.

"Nicely done, everybody," Michael heard the leader say. Then he was being hauled to his feet again and dragged across the rocky earth. Since they had driven up a rough hill to reach the wall, Michael had assumed they were at the bottom, but when they marched him a hundred yards along it, he was surprised to find himself on a ledge which revealed, far below, an immense pit which had been dug at the base of the wall.

Michael was horrified to see the nature of the industry that took place there.

At the base of the drop-off, there was an enormous pile of corpses, and another pile of skulls and bones. The gulch led to a building that looked like a cluster of teapots made of mud brick and stone, with a big pipe leading up to a cluster of buildings high on the wall. Like the children in the street, Michael saw lines and gangs of workers, only instead of carrying buckets, they were carrying bodies. The workers methodically processed their dead, sluicing them into the rotting pools, where the gasses of their decomposition—which Michael could easily identify on the hot breeze—could be gathered and used for fuel.

"It's a retirement job for the weak and sick," the Savior leader said with pride. "Anyone who dies down there can be carried just a few feet in order to be turned into fuel for the camp and feed for the other workers. Now that's efficiency."

"Where does the fuel go?" Michael said.

The Savior pointed to the distant lines of a graceful lodge perched high up on the hill, far from the stench of the dead. "The Madame's place, of course. When the wall finally falls, she'll be the first to see our world flood across all of Shook, expanding her domain to encompass everything beneath the putrid sky." The Savior patted

Michael on the back. "But you won't have to worry about that."

He turned him around. "Have a look here, Spirit Man," he said. Michael was now facing a broad swatch of the wall that had been smeared with white paint and streaks of red that could only have been blood. Here and there, blackened bullet holes pockmarked the rough-hewn stones. "This is the end of the road for you, Spirit Man. Your final stop. Must be a relief after all your struggling, eh? To finally have a chance to rest for all eternity."

Something about the place struck a profound sense of dread into Michael. Through his enhanced vision, he could see the wispy remnants of Visionaries who had stood before this wall and were extinguished forever. Something about this place was not like the rest of Shook.

"This is where my people die," Michael said, and felt Spirit Man speaking through him with such a deep sadness that he felt his legs might give way.

"Now you're catching on," the Savior said. "This is where your people die. And now, at long last, you'll be able to join them."

The roar of a powerful engine and the sound of skidding tires caught his ear. Michael turned to see a black limousine veer to a stop before him. Two Saviors ran over, opened the back door, and bowed deeply. To the blaring of retinue of assorted horns, a woman stepped from the car and coolly descended, gazing directly into Michael's eye with the greatest of disdain.

"Magellan!" he gasped. There she stood, dressed in a black funeral garb, her face full of gleeful contempt.

"Michael," she said, striding toward him. She spoke his name as if surprised to see him, as if he were an old friend she ran into unexpectedly at an office party. "How delightful of you to join us. I'm so glad you received my invitation."

"Magellan, what are you doing?"

"Don't call me that!" she snapped. She slapped him hard across the face, gave him a second to react, then slammed him backhanded across the other cheek. "Never. You will call me Madame or you will call me nothing at all. Actually, I think I prefer the latter."

"But...I trusted you."

She shrugged. "More's the pity. You ought to know better than anyone that Shook is an ever-shifting place. You can't even trust yourself in a place like this. I am sorry, though. I detest lying, but it seemed the only way to bring you to my doorstep. And here you are."

"Why are you doing this when you have such a beautiful life with your father?"

She waved his question away as if it were utterly inane. "Beautiful? I grew tired of 'beautiful' years ago. Now, no more questions."

She snapped her fingers and, at the command, the Savior holding Michael threw him to the ground and began kicking him in the belly and ribs again and again. Finally, Magellan brushed the Savior aside and knelt to put her hand under Michael's chin.

Holding his head up, she said, "I'm going to kill you now." Then she gestured and the Savior pulled Michael once more to his feet. The man dragged him to the white wall and pushed him against it.

"Prepare the firing squad," Magellan said to a nearby Savior, who immediately ran off. She stepped toward Michael again. "Sorry about the view," she said, gesturing at the vast field of abject suffering. "It's not exactly the note you want to go out on, I know, but this spot has a rather special quality, so you see we must do it here. Don't ask me why, but when a Visionary dies here, they don't come back. Then we throw their body into the processor with the rest and are done with them forever. So take heart in that, at least. After your gone, you'll become an extra little boost of protein so these workers can chip away at this behemoth for another day. An admirable contribution to the cause."

A dozen Saviors arrived at the wall with assault rifles and took their positions. Michael stared at them. He couldn't believe this was actually happening. After all this, all his struggles, everything he'd gone through to get here—was it all really going to end this way? Once again he scanned the eyes behind the masks, and once again he found not an ounce of compassion or forgiveness, not a flicker of guilt for what they were about to do. He looked to Magellan and

   VISION OF THE SPIRIT MAN

saw the same. No humanity in those eyes. He was ashamed by how easily he'd been duped. He reached inward, seeking the power of one of his spirit forms, but found only a fuzzy void, like TV static. Magellan was right, then. There was something truly different about this place.

Desperate for time, though he didn't know exactly how it would do him any good, Michael said, "Wait, don't I get some sort of last request? Or a last meal?"

Magellan laughed. "Our little candlelit dinner will have to be your last meal. I'm too impatient to let you choke down anything else. As for a last request, let me think….Oh, no." She turned to one of the Saviors, the leader who had first captured Michael. "Colonel, when the shadow arrives, execute the Spirit Man."

The Savior nodded and relayed the order to his men.

"What the hell is the shadow?" Michael said.

"Oh, don't worry your empty little head about it," Magellan said. "Just a tool to make sure you stay dead. I can't tell you how much we're all looking forward to this."

"Give me a cigarette," she said to nobody in particular. A shorter Savior immediately produced a pack of imported Turkish Dromedary Lights from his pocket and popped one out for her. A second Savior scurried forward with a lighter. Magellan took a long drag, then leaned on the hood of the black limousine. With a huge sigh, she let the smoke gush out from her mouth and nose in a swirling cloud. It wrapped itself around her and then drifted away on the wind.

"I do wish we'd timed this a little better," she said. "Waiting is so terribly boring, and you all know how I hate boring."

"Of course, Madame," the Colonel said. "I apologize for the over-sight, Madame."

"Well, nothing for it. I just hope the shadow doesn't take its sweet time in getting here." She exhaled another plume of smoke and, seeming to tire of the cigarette already, flicked it to the ground and stomped on it with surprising violence.

For a time, the sun seemed to stand still, and the heat grew more intense despite the perpetual smog cloud which hung over the land.

Magellan kept looking up at the sky, impatient. Then everything seemed to grow quieter, as if the world itself were receding to some distant place, making way for another reality. The sky began to darken.

"Oh thank god," Magellan said.

A breath of wind came up, and then a swirl, and then a burst which picked up the dust and drove it against the wall, carrying with it the stench of filth and blood and decay which pervaded the awful encampment. Magellan delicately pulled a black handkerchief from her pocket and held it against her nose. In seconds, a dark cloud began to pour over the top of the wall. Blue-white lightning flared within it but never touched down. Thunder rumbled from it like a low, constant growl. The sound swelled and swelled until it began to shake the earth itself. Michael saw part of the wall's scaffolding collapse some ways off and listened to the screams of the workers as they plunged to their deaths in the pit below.

The Colonel nodded at Magellan, who smiled at Michael.

"Well, it seems our time has come to an end, dear," she said. "I'd say it was nice knowing you, but, well, we both know that isn't true."

"Take aim but don't fire until I tell you to," the Colonel shouted to his troops.

All of them braced their rifles against their shoulders, flipped off the safeties, and leveled them straight at Michael's chest. The cloud stopped directly above them all and slowly began reshaping its chaotic mass into a circle. Deep in its shadow, Michael could see only silhouettes of the others. Something was bothering him, beyond the obvious immediate situation. Something was missing here.

"What about Annihilator?" Michael shouted at Magellan. "Who is it? And where?"

A flash of anger crossed her face but she quickly contained it. "Oh, that," she said. "To tell you the truth, we're still looking. But once you're out of the way, who's going to stop us? All things in due time."

Michael looked up at the wall towering above him. The cloud had nearly perfected its new shape. The lightning within was no longer sporadic and random, but a constant string of arcing electricity

     VISION OF THE SPIRIT MAN

which formed an arcane pattern that struck fear into a deep part of Michael's unconscious. *Dream killer,* came Spirit Man's voice from within. Michael swallowed hard but tried to keep his focus. He recalled the poem from the castle, one set of lines in particular:

A city of dreamers

can build a wall in a day or tear

it down in an instant

if only they know who they are

Who had built the wall, anyway? Who could have erected such an impenetrable structure overnight?

"Ready!" the Colonel bellowed.

He recalled the deep sadness in Emmitt's eyes when the soldier told him he knew who Annihilator was, and who needed to be destroyed.

"Aim!"

His thoughts turned then to the lush world he had glimpsed when he first began this journey, the life practically bursting from the earth in every direction. Wasn't that force more powerful than anything else? Wasn't it true, as the orb said, that life would prevail?

The cloud ahead perfected its circle. The killing symbol became clear as day, shining down upon him with a cold, cruel light. Just as the Colonel was about to bring down his arm and issue the order to fire, Michael spoke Annihilator's true name.

"Michael Seymour," he said. Then he shouted it at the wall and the sky and whatever else would listen. "My name is Michael Seymour!"

The Colonel froze. Magellan frowned. For a moment nothing happened. Then an immense crack tore up the wall, starting where Michael stood and zig-zagging up the immense structure with impossible speed, sending torrents of rocks and boulders careening toward the ground. One such boulder crashed directly in front of Michael, instantly pulverizing the entire firing squad and the Colonel. Magellan shrieked as the deadly hail rained down and dove back into her car.

"Go!" she screamed at her driver. "Go!"

Michael managed to squeeze out of his bindings, dove out of the way of a falling spike, and snatched up the Colonel's assault rifle, left abandoned just beyond the reach of his crushed fingers. Michael aimed directly at the back seat of the limousine and for a moment, their eyes met. He had a perfect bead. One squeeze of the trigger and The Madame would receive her just desserts for all the pain and misery she had inflicted on the people of Shook. Time seemed to freeze. Magellan's eyes went wide and she clearly expected a bullet to tear through her skull in the very next second. Michael's finger hovered over the trigger.

Then he moved it away and dropped the gun at his feet. No violence for vanity's sake. No violence unless it served a greater cause. He had already done what he came here to do.

Once the crack reached the top of the wall, a tremendous groan emanated from the structure, the structure which Michael himself had dreamed up without knowing it. The earth shuddered, and a huge section of the wall began to collapse entirely, sending an immense shockwave of debris bursting outward.

Michael ran.

He dodged falling rubble as he ran, desperately trying to outpace the wall of debris that was closing in with every passing second. In the distance, laborers and Saviors alike scrambled for shelter as the deadly downpour splattered red brains from the skull of anyone caught out in the open. The scaffolding on the wall crumbled entirely, sending all of its occupants to a quick death below. Michael knew he couldn't outrun the collapse, and looked around frantically for some other option.

Suddenly, from the clouded sky above, a rickety biplane appeared, wavering on the turbulent currents of air. It seemed to spot Michael and soared down toward him. He was prepared to fight off whoever might be aboard, but he saw, as it drew closer, that the pilot was none other than Captain Baylor of Fort Huachuca. The captain waved frantically as he approached and Michael nodded, hoping he understood. Then Michael angled so he was running in exactly the same direction as the plane was flying, as if he were attempting to flee from it. He listened, over the tumult of the collapsing

     VISION OF THE SPIRIT MAN

wall, and heard it getting closer and closer. Finally, just as it soared overhead, he leapt up and grabbed onto its landing gear. He swayed dangerously for a moment and nearly slipped, but then a hand reached down and helped him up into the cockpit.

"Wasn't sure I'd ever see you again, Spirit Man," Baylor said.

"Me either," said Michael. "I think you just saved my life though, so thank you."

"Don't thank me yet, kid, we've still got a ways to go before we're in the clear."

As if on cue, a wave of debris washed over them, pitching the plane sharply to the left and pelting Michael with pebbles. Baylor yanked hard on the throttle and managed to pull them high enough to regain control. They soared over the ongoing destruction, and Michael watched what looked like an unimaginable earthquake tear the whole rotting camp to pieces. Factories imploded, children shrugged off their burdens and fled.

"It's the end of the universe!" Baylor shouted, his voice thick with despair. "I know you tried your best, Spirit Man, and I don't blame you for what's about to happen. But damn, I didn't want to see all of Shook fall to the same sickness as the badlands."

Michael shook his head. "No, that's just the thing, Captain. That's not going to happen! I finally figured it out."

"The hell are you talkin' about? The wall has fallen, all is lost!"

"Not quite," Michael said. "Just watch."

Then the section of the wall where, moments ago, Michael had stood awaiting his execution, collapsed entirely, sending heaps of rubble and dust flowing across the land in an endless deluge of jagged, broken stone.

Chapter 16

A great silence fell upon the badlands at first, as the dust and debris settled. Michael stared across the wasteland, fingers crossed, and willed something to happen. For a while, nothing did.

"What am I s'pose to be seeing?" Baylor said. He banked the plane to circle the wreckage below.

"There," Michael said, pointing at the spot where the wall between the badlands and the rest of Shook had been entirely destroyed. The land was moving, changing. But instead of the sickness of the badlands spreading out to claim the rest of the dream world, as everyone had been so certain would happen, what occurred was quite the opposite. The lush greens and blues of Shook, the vibrant grasses and wildflowers and lakes and trees—all the colors of life— rushed through the break in the wall like a flood through the break in a dam. It poured across the badlands, washing away the Charnel House, washing away the black stone and the petrified trees, washing away the fetid pools and the toxic mist. In its place, the tremendous wave left blooming, bursting, insatiable life, emerging from every nook and cranny, turning that wasted, hopeless place into the fertile paradise it had once been.

"What am I looking at?" Baylor said, watching awestruck as the badlands transformed before his very eyes.

"Life prevailing," Michael said.

Baylor tried to keep himself composed for a moment, but couldn't hold it together. He began weeping tears of joy over the side of the plane. Those tears fell hundreds of feet to the earth and helped to water the new soil. Where each tear fell, a brilliant blue flower sprouted and turned its petals to the sun, which even now was emerging from the gray pall of clouds for the first time in anyone's memory. The unnatural clouds fled as the shattered ground was repaired, until the sky, too, had been healed.

"How did you know?" Baylor said. "How did you know this would happen?"

"I've learned some important lessons since I left your fort," Michael said. "This just happened to be one of them."

The dead Saviors and their dead slaves who, just moments before, had littered the wreckage of the Charnel House, sank into and were absorbed by the dirt. Roots found their way into the bodies and microbes worked overtime to break them down and reform them. Moments later, trees of all varieties—ash and sycamore and birch and oak and elm and willow and every other kind under the sun—grew from every spot where a body had fallen. Michael found himself wondering if Magellan had escaped the same fate as her Saviors. If she had not, which of those trees had she become? He picked out a tall, regal pine which looked just right. He nodded to it as if it might notice, and hoped Magellan found some peace in whatever her next life may have been. The sting of her betrayal had not left him, but he found it impossible to hold a grudge while watching the world come alive beneath him. He turned back to Baylor.

"Just think," he said. "Your children will grow up here, in this magnificent place. They will play with the deer and run through meadows and pick wildflowers to put in their hair. The badlands will exist only as a story told by their parents and grandparents."

Baylor shook his head. "I don't think I'll tell 'em about the badlands. Too much pain in that place."

"I understand, but I hope you'll reconsider. I think knowing what their home once was will help them to appreciate it all the more, and help make sure they never again allow the sickness to take over."

"Aye, there's wisdom in that yet." Baylor laughed. "Y'know, Spirit Man, I might've underestimated you. I took ya for nothin' but a hired gun, but you're more like a...well, I don't exactly know what I'd call ya."

"Me either, Captain. Me either."

As Michael watched, a line of pilgrims formed at the break in the wall, traveling from great distances to reach the paradise that was once called the badlands. The line started small, but soon stretched for miles. At Michael's suggestion, Baylor did a flyover to get a closer look. There were people from every part of Shook and all walks of life, soldiers and merchants and sailors and farmers and just about everything else Michael could think of. Some merchants walked up and down the long line of migrants, offering delicious foods and marvelous trinkets to tide the travelers over while they waited.

"Think I ought to take us back to Fort Huachuca," Baylor said. "Plane's runnin' a bit low on fuel."

"Wait," Michael said. "Just set me down somewhere near here. I want to see this up close."

"Anything for you, Spirit Man."

Moments later, Baylor found a narrow strip of flat land and touched down. Michael hopped out and helped him spin the plane around so it could take off again using the same runway.

"Well, Spirit Man, I suppose this is goodbye."

Michael nodded. "But probably not forever. Whoever knows in this place?"

"I hope you're right. But before ya go, I jus' thought I should say…" He swallowed hard, then continued. "Emmitt was a good soldier and a better man. He'd be damn proud of what you did today, I jus' know it."

"Thank you, Captain Baylor. That means a lot to me."

Then Baylor saluted, Michael saluted back, and the captain was off, sailing back into the sky in his fixer-upper of a plane. Michael watched the rickety vessel soar off until it disappeared over the wall, then he turned and joined the stream of pilgrims.

"Excuse me," he said to a woman carrying a baby on her back. "This place through the wall—what do people call it?"

"Why, they call it the Valley of the Phoenix."

Michael smiled. "That's a good name."

"I certainly think so." Then she waved and melted back into the crowd. Michael walked along the long line, marveling at how quickly news of this new paradise had spread, and how eager people were to venture into it. Then he wondered how many of these people had been there, or had family or ancestors there, before it became the badlands in the first place. How many had fled for years, and only now were able to return to their homeland? Michael felt a warm giddiness rising inside him. It was all worth something, in the end. All the fighting, all the blood spilled. It actually made a difference.

Of course it did, came Spirit Man's voice. *That's what we're here for. The right man in the right place.*

Spirit Man walked with the crowd as they shuffled through the gap that was once a wall. To his surprise, he found a city there, perched where the slave camp had once been. But this city, of course, was entirely different. Gleaming skyscrapers reached high into the air. People bustled here and there through the streets. Trees sprouted from every sidewalk and even from the sides of buildings. Birds chirped from every direction, singing to their hearts' content. Michael strode down the streets in awe, amazed at the simple fact of all these ordinary people going about their ordinary lives. A group of children passed on bicycles, ringing little bells to let other pedestrians know of their approach. A man tried on a tuxedo in one shop window while, across the street, a woman tried on a wedding dress. Both were beaming.

Despite the fact that Michael had never before been to this city, and in fact had no idea how it had been constructed and populated so quickly, he felt innately familiar with every street, every address. It was as if the whole thing had been stamped on his brain before its creation, and he was only now recognizing patterns which had been in his head all along. He passed a newspaper stand and, unable to resist, stopped by and picked up a copy. The front page story read: "Famed Poet Jacques Champs Releases First Collection in Decades." The story, which detailed Jacques's new poetry collection, was accompanied by a photograph of the poet himself, smiling at his desk with the vast ocean visible through the windows behind him. Michael was glad that he, at least, had survived the day's events.

Without realizing it, Michael turned onto a street he knew perfectly from his childhood. It felt almost completely out of place amid the skyscrapers, given that it was a New Mexico suburb populated almost entirely by adobe, one-story homes. A street sign at the corner read "Seymour Lane." Cautious and curious, he walked down it, gripped by nostalgia at the sight of all the houses he had passed nearly every day in his youth. At the end of the road, as he knew he would find, was Mark's house. A little white house with green trim and a cheerful green door. At first, Michael did not want to approach. He knew what awaited him, and he didn't know if he could face it. But he looked around at the city and drew strength from all the good that was possible. Then he approached the house.

Michael knocked gently, half hoping no one would answer. Footsteps approached from the other side. Mark opened the door, as young as he had been when he died in Michael's arms.

"Michael!" he said. "I didn't know if you were gonna show. Come in, come in." He waved Michael inside and Michael had no choice but to accept the invitation. The house was exactly as he remembered it, sparsely but tastefully decorated, a few hanging plants here, some pewter figurines on the windowsill there. The door slid shut behind him.

Mark pulled a beer from the fridge and cracked it open. "Want one?" he said, offering it to Michael.

"Uh, no thanks. I don't think I can stay long."

"I know, man. I know."

Mark sat on the couch and motioned for Michael to take the leather chair opposite him.

"Weird, right?" Mark said. "How long's it been since you came over here?"

"I don't know. Years. Years since I've even thought about it. I try not to, mostly."

"Yeah, I can understand that. I'm glad you came, though. There's something I need to tell you."

"I already know," Michael said, waving him off. "I know it was my fault. I think about it every single day, even all these years later.

If I could have just pulled myself together, if I hadn't—"

Mark cut him off. "No, man, that's not it at all. That's not what I need to tell you. What I need to tell you is…you've got to let it go. You've got to let me go. Stop beating yourself up over this—no one could've known some dumb argument at a bar would end with a knife in my gut. And look, listen. I pushed you out of the way because I wanted to. Not because of anything you did. I did it because I wanted you to live. You understand?"

Michael nodded. His mouth was dry and he could push any words through his lips.

"Then *live*, man," Mark said. "I knew what I was doing. That's not a burden for you to carry around all your life. It's a gift. And, judging by what I see here in what people used to call the badlands, it looks like you're making pretty excellent use of that gift."

"It doesn't change what happened."

"No, no it doesn't. But if you can't let go of that, if you can't forgive yourself for that, you'll lose sight of everything you do change. That's all I'm saying. Enough dwelling on death. Lie down in some grass, sniff some roses, focus on life. You got me?"

"I think so," Michael said.

"Great, because my time's just about up here." He stood and brushed himself off, then looked Michael in the eye. "And hey, it was great seeing you, man."

And just like that, he was gone. Michael was sitting alone in a dark, empty house. He stood and looked around. He ran his finger over the mantle and it came away caked in dust. He picked up the picture that rested there—Michael and Mark after a long, hard hike, both sweating but smiling broadly, arms draped around each other's shoulders. If their faces hadn't been quite so different, anyone could have mistaken them for brothers. Michael set the photo down and left the house.

Instead of emerging into the city, however, he found himself stepping into the Wanderer's Diner. The place was trashed. The windows were all shot out and bullet holes marred the walls and counters. There was broken glass everywhere, and every surface and object was splattered with blood. But it was full of diners, who were themselves bloody and all shot up. They didn't seem to notice, however. They just sat in their booths or at the counter and kept on eating, sipping their coffee, and making lighthearted conversation, totally oblivious to the fact that their clothing was torn and soaked in blood, and bits of tattered flesh hung from their ragged wounds.

The scene was jarringly horrible, grotesque, and yet the atmosphere of amiable cheer made it seem like a parody of disaster, a crude imitation of the real thing. Michael looked to the booth where he remembered sitting. The only person missing from the scene was Mark. He'd vanished as if he was never there at all.

Wendy approached Michael, her faced caked in dried blood that cracked when she smiled.

"Have a seat right in that booth over there and I'll be right with you," she said, motioning to the booth where Michael had sat that morning...or whatever morning it was. He had a hard time keeping the timeline straight. When was the shooting, anyway? Was that before or after Fort Huachuca? Not knowing what else to do, he sat at the booth and browsed the menu. It was full of gibberish. Nonsense collections of letters and numbers and childish scribbles that amounted to nothing at all.

"Are we ready to order?" Wendy said, pen and pad in hand.

"Uh, sure, can I just get a cup of coffee?" Michael said.

"Coming right up." Wendy whirled and disappeared into the kitchen. When Michael looked up again, there was a strange man sitting across from him. Michael jumped in surprise but the man put out a hand to calm him.

"Whoa there, Spirit Man," he said. "Hold your horses now."

Wendy returned with a coffee for Michael and a plate of pancakes for the stranger.

"Enjoy," she said.

"Many thanks, Wendy," said the man. Then he dug into his meal.

"Who are you?" Michael said. "Have I met you before?"

"Oh, you never know. Maybe. Name's Lohman, John Lohman. I'm the janitor here."

Michael leaned in close and glanced at the other patrons conspiratorially. None of them seemed to be listening in on him, but he didn't want to be overheard nonetheless.

"Are we all...dead?" he said.

Lohman shook his head and swallowed a mouthful of pancakes. He reached for the syrup.

"Nope," he said. "I'm not dead. I was in the bathroom unclogging a toilet when I heard the gunshots, so, hero that I am, I just stayed in there. It seemed to work out all right in the end."

"I'm not sure I'd go that far," Michael said.

"Well, we'll see, now won't we? Now, why don't you tell me something about yourself. How come your dreams are so violent and angry?"

"What's it to you?"

"Well, seeing as I'm liable to get caught in them, I think I have a right to know."

Michael slouched into his seat and said, "Well, maybe it's because I'm dying."

"Aren't we all?" clucked Lohman. "You should read the obituaries. Every day you'll find someone who's just died. Most days a whole lot more than just one."

"Okay, sure, but I mean for real."

"Another matter of perspective," Lohman said.

"You're not being very helpful."

Lohman shrugged. "It's not my job to be helpful. It's my job to clean up after you. Make sure you think about all the little messes you leave behind."

"I thought you said you were the janitor here?"

"I can have more than one job, can't I?" Lohman licked his fingers and set his utensils down on the now-empty plate. "Now, tell me, Spirit Man. What do you think happened here?"

Michael looked around at all the mutilated, bloody patrons. "I came in here with Mark for lunch," he said. "And some crazy dickhead came in with a gun and blew everybody away."

"Okay, so how do you feel about that?" Lohman said.

"What kind of a stupid question is that? How do I feel? How the hell do you think I feel?"

"So we're gonna go with: pretty angry."

Michael folded his arms. "I don't see the point of any of this."

As soon as he said it, he noticed someone to Lohman's left—someone he knew hadn't been there before. Joey, the gunman. He sat there, dazed, tear-streaked, hollowed by hunger and fear. He didn't move, didn't speak, just stared at Michael.

"Is this the guy?" Lohman said casually.

Michael, struggling to control his fight or flight response, said, "Yes."

"So, hypothetically, if you had this guy right in front of you, and you had a gun in your hand..."

"I don't have a—" Before Michael could finish his sentence he felt a new weight in his right hand. He looked down and saw a fully loaded 9mm pistol resting there. The safety was off.

"So," Lohman went on. "As I was saying: If you had this guy right in front of you and you had a gun in your hand and the whole damn crowd he just cut down was watching you, what would you do?"

Michael looked around the diner and realized all the patrons were gathered around him now, eagerly awaiting his next move. He looked from face to face and on all of them he saw fear, but he also saw rage. Without needing to hear a word, he knew they wanted him to pull the trigger. He could practically hear them in his head, chanting, *Make him pay! Make him pay!*

Michael looked at Lohman. He looked at Joey. He looked at the gun in his hand. Then he flipped on the safety, ejected the magazine, and slammed the gun in front of Lohman.

"Go to hell," he said.

Lohman smiled. "Good choice, Spirit Man. I'll see you around."

With that, the whole world twisted in on itself, emitted a static *pop*, and disappeared.

Chapter 11

Michael Seymour felt himself being shaken awake. He looked up into the face of a young waitress. "Sir? Sir, you'll have to wake up," she said. "We're closing now." He rubbed his eyes and glanced at the red plastic tag pinned to her uniform, where "Wanda" was written with a permanent marker in swirling cursive.

"Oh, I'm sorry. I guess I fell asleep," he said. He looked around. The diner was empty and intact. No blood, no bodies, no bullet holes.

"Did I come in here alone?" he said.

"Sure did," she said. "You came in about two hours ago, ordered a hamburger, and fell asleep without eating it. I can bring you another, if you want it."

"No, thanks," he said. "I feel like all I've been doing is eating, and... well, never mind. I should get going anyway." He stood, fished in his pocket for a twenty-dollar bill and handed it to Wanda, saying, "Keep the change, thanks."

Michael walked out into the late afternoon light, headed for the bus stop. Trekking along the side of the dusty road, he couldn't shake the memories of all those similar treks in Shook, wandering for what seemed like years through a featureless expanse of sand and dust. Was it really possible that all of that had taken place in only two hours? Even though it was the most rational explanation, he couldn't quite believe it. Everything had been too real, he had felt everything too sharply, for all of that to be nothing but stories his synapses told him in his sleep.

He heard a familiar mechanical buzzing and looked off into the desert to see a couple of guys zooming around on dune buggies, kicking up clouds of dust as they careened in circles, jumping over small ditches, and laughing as they did so, having just a grand old time. No machine guns, no masks, no tanks in the distance. Michael walked on. A truck passed with its windows down and the radio blasting some talk show. The voice, though he heard it for only a second before it vanished, was unmistakable.

"Magellan?" he said, watching the green truck speed away into the shimmering distance. He shook his head. Was he losing it? Was he just going crazy out here in the desert, seeing dead people and hearing voices that never existed? But, reflecting on the way everything turned out in the dream world, he decided it wasn't the worst way in the world to go crazy. At least the good guys won in the end.

Finally, Michael reached the bus stop and dropped himself heavily onto the little metal bench. He had no idea what time it was or what time the next bus to Las Cruces was supposed to arrive, but after spending so long in Shook, time just didn't seem especially important. It was such a fickle, uncertain thing, after all, so what was the use in trying to pin it down? Better to just let it flow however it liked, grabbing on when you could and letting go when it became too slippery.

There was one thing he couldn't quite figure out, sitting there alone at that bus stop in the middle of nowhere. And that was: how the hell did he get out here if no one drove him? His car wasn't in the parking lot, and he sure as hell didn't remember taking the bus, but the waitress had said he'd come in completely alone. He tossed the thought around for a while but couldn't come up with a reasonable answer. Either he was just having a pretty severe forgetful spell and should consider getting it checked out by a head doctor, or something more had happened, something that couldn't be explained away as nothing but some crazy bunch of dreams. Given the usual content of those dreams, Michael wasn't sure if he found that latter idea comforting or terrifying. Eventually he settled on "both" because it felt most appropriate.

After a while—Michael wasn't sure how long and still had no desire to check the time—another passenger showed up at the bus stop and sat on the opposite end of the bench. Michael barely glanced at him as he first sat down, but something about the newcomer drew

     VISION OF THE SPIRIT MAN

his eye again. There was something familiar about the man. He was ragged and weather-worn, with a general down-on-his-luck sort of look to him. His beard was long and unkempt, as was the greasy hair that ran down to the nape of his neck. Something deep inside Michael told him he needed to start a conversation with this man, just open his mouth and say something so the man would respond. After a few moments of hesitation, he finally decided to give in to the strange impulse.

"Excuse me," he said. "Do you have the time, by any chance?"

The man looked up at him and grinned. Michael knew he knew that face, those crooked teeth, those deep-set eyes, but couldn't quite place it.

"Sure thing, stranger," the man said. He reached into his pocket and pulled out a rusty old pocket watch that looked like it had come from an entirely different era. He flipped it open and laughed.

"Whoops, sorry man," the stranger said. "I completely forgot that this thing actually broke years and years back. Guess I don't have much use for keeping time, most days."

"Oh, I know that feeling," Michael said. "Don't worry about it, I'm sure the bus will get here soon."

"Maybe," said the man. "Maybe not. The way I see it, if it gets here, it's supposed to be here. If it doesn't, it's supposed to be somewhere else. The world just makes more sense if you look at it that way, if you look at it and think everything and everyone always lands exactly where they're supposed to be."

Michael raised an eyebrow. "I think I've heard someone say something like that before," he said. "Just...about a different place. Not here." He extended his hand. "I'm Michael, by the way. Michael Seymour."

"Nice to meet you, Michael. I'm Joey. Just Joey."

Michael kept his smile on, but felt a deep unease at the name. Joey. Joey with the gun. Joey with the tears streaming down his face. Joey with the gun. Joey with the blood. Joey behind the mask of the Saviors. Michael peered down the road and wondered, for the first time, what the hell was taking the bus so long. He suddenly had a desperate need to get as far away from here as possible, and even considered running across the desert—though he knew how foolish that would be.

"Where you headed, Michael?" Joey said.

"Home," Michael said. "Honestly, I'm just excited to get home and see my friends again."

"You been away long?"

"Yes and no. It's complicated, but it feels like it's been a very, very long time. How about you? Where's the road taking you today?"

"Today?" Joey snorted. "Who knows. Just a warm bed for now. Tomorrow, though, that's the real question. Place like this, all open air..." He gestured out at the desert around them, the vast silence of it, the hidden life huddled in every shadow and under every rock. "The way I see it, there's a lot of paths you can take. I see some of them and I know I don't want those. I see others and I think, maybe. But do you want to know the ones I'm really after?"

"Which ones are those?"

Joey grinned, once more showing his crooked teeth. "I want to follow the paths I can't see. The ones that aren't laid out for me yet. Because I don't much like where all the others go. I don't like the places where they take me."

Michael nodded. He felt like Joey was getting at something much vaster than what he was saying, but he couldn't put his finger on exactly what that was. So he didn't say anything in reply. He just turned and looked back across the desert, where a dusk breeze had started to blow. Michael and Joey sat there, side by side at the bus stop, as sunlight retreated from that empty world. They sat there in the cool night air, waiting for the bus to arrive, waiting for some pair of headlights to show them the way forward.

     VISION OF THE SPIRIT MAN

ABOUT THE AUTHOR

George Mendoza

George Mendoza was born in New York City in 1955. At the age of 15, he was diagnosed with a rare, incurable, degenerative eye disease, fundus flavimaculatus. Effects of the disease caused him to lose his central vision, keeping only a gray foggy fringe on the periphery. In the center of his view, he sees what he calls "kaleidoscope eyes"—intense and changing visual images of fiery suns, brightly burning eyes; and colorful pinwheels. These spectacles almost never leave him, not even when he lays down in darkness to go to sleep.

A man of vision and courage, George went on to become a world-class runner and Paralympic contender. In 1980, he broke the world record for blind athletes, running the mile in 4 minutes and 28 seconds. In the early 1990's, he began to paint full-time. Ironically, Mendoza's paintings spring from the loss of his eyesight and a very special vision that took its place. He had grown increasingly frustrated by his dancing colors, which would not leave him alone. He spoke to a priest at the Holy Cross Retreat House in New Mexico. "Paint them," the priest said. "Make designs, pictures from them."

George Mendoza remembers physical sight, and so his works derive from visual memories intertwined with dreams, visions, and emotional experiences, meaning Mendoza paints both figuratively and abstractly. His work then transcends the physical world, exploring the spiritual, the mystical, the playful, and sometimes the darker nuances of the human spirit.

Mendoza works full time as a writer and an artist. Currently, his exhibition "Colors of the Wind" is a national Smithsonian affiliates traveling art exhibit. He lives in Las Cruces, New Mexico, and is founder and president of the Wise Tree Foundation, Inc., a nonprofit corporation for the promotion for the arts. He is a motivational speaker and is currently developing a play based on his children's book *Colors of the Wind*, a biography of his life written by J.L. Powers and illustrated using Mendoza's artwork.

Learn more at www.georgemendoza.com.

www.ingramcontent.com/pod-product-compliance
Lightning Source LLC
Chambersburg PA
CBHW020116310726
48970CB00002B/658